T0356183

Stealing Faith

Stealing Faith

Leora Skolkin-Smith

THE
STORY
PLANT

The Story Plant
1270 Caroline Street
Suite D120-381
Atlanta, GA 30307

Copyright © 2023 by Leora Skolkin-Smith
The Library of Congress Cataloguing-in-Publication Data is available upon request.

Story Plant hardcover ISBN-13: 978-1-61188-331-2
Story Plant e-book ISBN-13: 978-1-945839-67-2

Visit our website at www.TheStoryPlant.com

First Story Plant Printing: September 2023

Printed in the United States of America
0 9 8 7 6 5 4 3 2 1

To Alexa and Niki

"How shall I seek the origin? where find Faith in the marvellous things which then I felt? Oft in these moments such a holy calm Would overspread my soul, that bodily eyes Were utterly forgotten, and what I saw Appeared like something in myself, a dream, A prospect in the mind."
—*The Prelude*, William Wordsworth

"leap of faith": noun
The act of believing in or accepting something outside
of the boundaries of reason—it is to believe in a sub-
jective truth about the meaning of life, to believe in
something that can't be truly seen in this world.
—Wikipedia

Chapter One.

August, 1988

Last night, I dreamed I was back in Faith Hale's apartment on West Tenth Street. I was young again in the dream, only twenty-five. "You can't die yet," I said to Faith in the dream, standing by her sick bed where she had been laid up with the cancer. "I have something to tell you." The door to Faith's bedroom was open. Light flooded in from the corridor. I was giving Faith my first novel about being in the mental hospital, and my pages were a confession of something, a weight of burden.

Awakened, I lifted the top sheet, slid out of the bed where my husband, Michael, would still be sleeping beside me if he hadn't gone to a medical conference in Akron this week. Quietly, I made my way through the dark kitchen to the lightless bathroom. This was all a familiar haunting.

I didn't turn the lights on when I reached the bathroom. The dark was where all my thoughts belonged, I told myself. I pulled off my flimsy summer nightgown and twisted the shower knob for a cold shower. The air conditioner wasn't on in the apartment; it wasn't working, and the dream had pulled sweat from my pores. The water poured from the shower, hitting the tub basin, and when my hand went out to feel it, the cold water felt too sharp, too harsh, and too cruel, so I quickly turned it off.

11

I took a dry towel from the rack, put it on the porcelain bed of the tub, and laid myself upon it. I rested inside the tub on my back, wearing only my underpants, staring mindlessly up into the shower head.

Outside was the same gray cobalt-blue skyline I remembered when I had spent days walking on the boardwalk beside the rushing FDR Drive, thinking I wanted to be on the streets like the other former psychiatric patients. I had slept on sterile beds, in common dorms, with the moans of "crazy people." I'd worn seclusion room clothes, clad in a strong dress from neck to thigh, and I hadn't felt anything or any person like my husband, Michael, holding me for all those many months.

There Faith was at dawn in August, 1988, fifteen years since my first incarceration, under a goose feather comforter on an old walnut wood bed, lying in her husband, Don's, austere farmhouse; deer skipping through sugar bush and grasses, barns, toolsheds, and rusted weathervanes, her family watching her. Faith was all bones and baldness now, living in a red barn of a house on a sprawling Vermont farm after seventy-nine years in New York City. The chemotherapy and radiation had stopped. Endless vitamins and vegetarian foods were given, the holistic measures Faith always supported, blending proclamations of the importance of people ingesting only natural, organic ingredients into her protests and speeches about men destroying the earth with their toxic chemicals and violence: Indian Point and Chernobyl. Just when her breasts needed curing, came the indignity that, in her end, it was man's chemicals that were prolonging her life. Her body swelling with seeds of cancer from her removed breast. Two years ago a man with a knife had removed the breast; its absence was haunting the rest of Faith.

A few tiny beads of water were shining on the steel head of the shower, clinging, and they wouldn't drop. Now it seemed everything was on the verge of pouring out, and there had been a relief in stopping it in the almost-dryness. Everything was dry, but I could not go back to bed. Hard and dark — the tub, the bathroom, my body, my feelings. I lay still and cool. My eyes ached. I didn't want the water to run, or the morning to come. I did not want to break again. I did not want to go back to the mental hospital.

Chapter Two.

I was nineteen years old and looking to be saved when I first met the famous author, Faith Hale. It was 1973, at Abigail Stone College, during a week of bleak, damp nights and daily rainstorms.

Faith Hale was known for staying late on campus if the weather was bad. Her beat-up 1971 Volkswagen was reputed to be filled with political protest pamphlets, books, and 'feminist' poems which were suspected of being radically lesbian, explicit, racy, and exciting. Some students said that Faith Hale was at the first bra-burning protests of the 1970s, and that she swung her bra overhead like a lasso and set the offending garment on fire. Students called Faith Hale "Mother Sugar". She had that effect. And I needed some sweetness now. She had been arrested and put in the House of Detention in the 1960s for protesting the draft for the Vietnam War by participating in sit-ins and holding banners in illegal places. She wrote of her fellow prisoners in jail after she was tried for civil disobedience: ". . .in my company, so many prostitutes and self-hurters who will never be heard. . ." I thought there was already something Faith Hale knew about me.

I ran in the cold rain, drenched so that my hatless head looked crowned by a whorl of wet hair. I was clutching the pages of my manuscript, which I had placed in a large green Hefty garbage bag to protect its pages. Before this, I had shown my manuscript to the famous left-wing novelist M.B. Dickers, who also taught at the school.

I might have never met Faith, nor have braved the downpour and the risk of humiliation from Faith, too, if Dickers hadn't fucked my best friend, Susan Hunt, in a motel room opposite the Howard Johnson on the Bronx River Parkway.

With the rain falling in my hair. I slowed down my pace and combed my hair with the fingers of my right hand. Droplets of rain made that hand look blistered as my mind wandered, thinking of M.B. Dickers.

He had looked kosher as a pickle, his round face amiable and unremarkable. He must be the friendly father of someone, I thought when I first registered for his class that September in 1973. He looked at me without seeing me, but I believed there was a kindness in his face; I was attracted to him. He smelled of the Mars bars and cupcakes from the campus canteen which he kept in his jacket pockets. His ordinary looks did not seduce me. It wasn't sex I wanted from him; I felt desperate for his attention to my writing. To have his famous hands on my written pages was my obsession for my whole first week at Abigail Stone. It felt like a flu had overtaken my body, that I had been stricken by inhaling the air around him.

When I saw Faith, it was different. I had seen Faith walking by me with students, heard fragments of their conversations; Faith's warm, lively voice coming back to me on the wind. I had a yearning to be one of those students close to Faith Hale, but it frightened me. I didn't know what kind of yearning that was. Even Faith's fingers seemed to be listening to whatever the students were saying, as Faith walked them up the hill to where all the writing faculty had offices.

The rain wasn't letting up. I wiped my wet hand against my jeans, thinking about Dickers's dismissal and how my despair had persisted for a long, tortuous week without relief. I had experienced the harshness of the late fall weather through the thin denim of my blue jeans, the shabby mohair sweaters I'd bought at a tag sale at Lawrence Hospital. I often walked on Pondfield Road, under the cement tunnel by the Bronxville railroad tracks, past the one luncheonette in the town, the "Bar and Bistro", the few small suburban clothing stores with expensive brand-name clothes, and the Italian restaurant that opened at five o'clock.

The town was tightly zoned and immaculate, and the wooden footbridges and Bronx River flowing into Manhattan held places of temporary peace for me, enclaves full of native trees—hornbeam, locust, and flowering dogwoods, deep green but unidentifiable shrubs. And there were ducks, mallards mostly, and Canadian geese. Against the long path of mudslide, bushes, and rhododendrons, I had thought about my father, killed in a riptide off the coast of Cape Elizabeth in Maine a few years ago when I was young, fully dressed in his summer sucker suit with his meticulously folded red silk handkerchief in its front pocket. His death had been pronounced a suicide because he was so scrupulously dressed and there had been no evidence nor other hand-prints nor 'blunt instrument' marks on his sacrificed body. He left no note behind.

Again I brushed my fingers through my wet hair and felt droplets roll onto my lips. I had waited in sleeplessness in my dorm room all week for Dickers to finally read my novel: sketches of myself, my father's suicide, my father and my mother, Sofia, and brother Julian and the abortion I had that summer, which I had tried to make fiction by adding things to the experience that didn't happen. I had sequestered myself in the big barn on my mother's estate, writing about the painful procedure which took an unformed fetus from within me. I saw it in a jar after—blood and placenta, floating in a briny liquid.

I tried to pick up my pace again. I did not want the "dark states" to come. The dark states were as bleak and brutal as a gala night in a graveyard. A virus in the soul, I called them. I would suddenly feel tightened and twisted, as if I were a drenched towel being wrung out by my own hands. They were there even before my father's death and the abortion. It's called "depressive", one of the doctors my mother took me to told me. "Do you hear your father calling you to join him often?" When I began my novel, I had ended a short affair with an older man I'd met who made me pregnant, a TV producer, when I did a walk-on part for the soap opera *The Edge of Night*. My mother had let me stay by myself in a room at the Barbizon in Manhattan and study acting at the Neighborhood Playhouse for a year after foundering at NYU for two years. But it all fell through once the abortion happened and the "dark states" descended so fiercely upon me.

The "dark states" fell on me like a toxic rain. I could not escape the darkness when it fell. I'd had the dark states more and more since the abortion, but I was certain that leaving acting and going to college would keep them at bay. This was why I ended up at Abigail Stone College.

Sometimes I had hoped that instead of the dark states, I would go mad. There was a porthole in my consciousness, I sometimes thought, and it led out. But it could be hours before I found it, before the darkness stopped swallowing me. It often felt as if I were an innocent adolescent girl who was constantly trying to purify herself of guilty thoughts by despairing of *everything*. The dark states obliterated guilty thoughts.

"A novel has three acts," Dickers had said when I finally gave him my pages. "Act One, Act Two, Act Three. You don't have any. You have some virtues as a writer, though; the dialogue is at least somewhat energetic." Then he had walked to the window, the beautiful bow window overlooking the tennis courts at Andrews, and I realized I was only his required task for the day. When he turned to see if I was still in the room after his brief bestowed words, he looked exasperated. He puffed up his cheeks and let out a long "poof" like a fart, not caring if I minded when it blew on me, and though it was for only a few degrading seconds, I thought again about suicide.

The rain was relentless; it seemed to pull my jeans as it licked them down, and for a second, almost halfway there to Andrews, I was suddenly afraid my pants would slide off, wet. And I felt a sharp panic.

Dickers. . .who did he think he was? I asked myself. Did he really feel that he wrote the brilliant prose people said he did? So. . .well? I had read about Dickers's "octopus" in his novel about a playland in Walt Disney World in which a fictional Walt Disney (whom Dickers's novel portrayed as a Neo-Nazi capitalist) kept a mechanical octopus for an audience seated in bleachers above a swimming pool. In the novel, a real live beauty queen was in the water with the octopus. A young innocent girl was watching from the audience as the octopus grabbed the woman with two of his electrically propelled metal tentacles and turned her around and around in the water, the tentacles probing and holding her. The scene ended with the woman's bathing suit floating solo in the swimming pool. And the woman, humiliated, naked in the pool, trying desperately to swim to shore.

Once, in my dreams, Dickers was pushing me onto my stomach, whisking up a skirt I was wearing, and seductively, slowly, mercilessly peeling my panties. Why was I having sex dreams about this terrible man? I woke up wet in my sex, with no exit to slip through to halt the crawling orgasm. Touching my clitoris, I rubbed out the poisonous condemnation: you are a dirty, bad girl. Then I brought myself into an orgasm so large it seemed to crack the overhanging sky. and the pieces of falling sky and my fantasy buried my shame under an ethereal rubble of blue. I knew Dickers slept with students.

The purpose of Susan Hunt's visit that evening had seemed suspicious. Susan had a glimpse of my stack of pages while in the dorm's lounge, and had inquired if it was a novel, and if so, what did Dickers say about it?

"He told me you gave him something of yours to read. What did he say to you about it?" Susan had asked me.

"Oh, he didn't like it. He just didn't," I said, wondering why I answered, and why I hadn't lied. Then I had the strength to remain still even as I swelled with regret for saying this out loud.

"I'm sorry, I think he told me that about your manuscript too. Right; he said it wasn't very good."

I was sure this was the reason for Susan's visit, but then I noticed Susan's slacks were noticeably loose and had ridden up on her lithe legs, exposing their light blond hairs and the ambiguous sexual intentions of her whole body. Susan lightly touched my right leg with her long fingers, smiling at me suggestively, and the room seemed to blur and pulse as she pulled her legs into a sitting Indian position on my unmade bed. I paused and silenced myself, worried that the possibility of sharing Dicker's dismissal of my pages and my humiliation in front of Susan would excite us both. I willed my own confession to dissipate instead, and then simply leave my mind and Susan's mind too, as if I had never said anything. I felt a sickening terror. I was afraid of something I didn't understand. I sat up straighter. But sudden lucidity and determination came back to me. My spine tightened. Hold on to yourself, I thought. Just hold on.

Susan Hunt stretched out one arm to beckon me to come sit with her by the pillow. She whipped out a Gauloises cigarette from a package in her back jean slacks' pocket. "I wouldn't say he was a bad lover, he wasn't much, though," Susan said, laughing, and went on, describing in detail how she had made love with Dickers, forcing me to envision Dickers's pot-bellied self on Susan's spoon-shaped, enviable body. But, thinking this, I was relieved of the unnamable fears. Susan wasn't going to touch me; Susan had only wanted to take pleasure of herself as I had told her about my failure with Dickers.

I let out an imprisoned breath. I dug myself under the sheets of my bed in despair after Susan left. I had lost my way again, I thought, and I tried to stifle the voice which called me a failure. A few nights before, I had dreamed again of the gentleman's barn on my mother's estate where I'd written that first novel about the abortion and these "dark states" that still sometimes overcame me, my father's voice calling me to join him now.

I lay immobile on my dorm room bed after seeing Susan. Until the moon outside my window seemed to shout at me to come out of it. And then something called me to go and see Faith Hale. And an hour after Susan Hunt left my dorm room, I had hustled to my desk and gathered up the 120 pages of my manuscript I had written in my mother's barn on the Bedford estate and placed it inside a Hefty garbage bag. The image of Faith Hale walking with her students swirled in my head like

a medicine, causing delirium but cure. I could not fail
again, I told myself, as I now hurried in the freezing rain
towards Faith's office. My long hair looked dead black,
the usual reddish-brown glints extinguished by the rain.
My olive skin coloring, which I had from my Argentinean mother, was pale from lack of sleep. And like
my father's, I knew my face seemed dramatic, acutely
alert, as if perpetually discerning an emergency calling
me from a distance.

I reached the grassy knoll that led upward to Andrews Manor where Faith's office was. Most of the rest
of the college was made up of a set of half-timbered
residences with brickwork, mullioned windows, and
dormers: a "Tudorbethan" campus, imitating medieval
castles and country houses with faceted staircase towers
and red roofs. The terrain of the campus was shaped
by dramatic outcroppings of exposed bedrock shaded by
large oak and elm trees.

The campus of Abigail Stone College was originally a
part of the estate of the college's founder, Thomas Stone.
He named the college after his feminist wife, Abigail
Harriet Stone, who died in 1926. The college was con-
structed by the transportation of mansions from different
estates in Bronxville by trucks and lorries. In 1924 Lydia
Booth's special interest in Vassar's "euthenics" program
— which supported the idea that the air and the environ-
ment would make young women "special" and ready for
"socialization" — inspired him to found a new college.
Vassar's faculty interest in euthenics dwindled when they
began to confuse euthenics with eugenics, and Abigail
Stone College was finally launched as an all women's
college. Abigail Stone became Vassar's rogue sister.

I stumbled toward Faith's office grasping onto the
Hefty bag. Through the rain, I could see the wooden
entrance door of Andrews. The colonial columns and

a lintel above the sharply arched entranceway were all painted white as toothpaste. I looked up. I knew the sun was somewhere out there in the drizzle and darkness, but I couldn't see it.

Andrews Manor seemed deserted now, its stucco and brickwork slick from the downpour. Scared, I slipped inside. All the offices were locked, but I could sit at the end of the lobby stairway and dry off. No, I wouldn't knock on Faith Hale's door to see if Faith was there, I decided suddenly. It was late and the building was empty anyway, and what was I thinking? Another humiliation to make things even worse?

The chandelier was the only light on in the vestibule, and shaking the rain out of my mohair sweater, I struggled through what to do, unsure if I really should knock on Faith's office door or stay on the stairs.

There was a deep quiet here, as if the high ceiling, fireplaces, and spiraling main staircase were in still meditation under the chandelier light. I decided to at least wait out the downpour, seating myself at the foot of the rickety colonial staircase again. In the near-darkness, the majestic vestibule comforted me and I felt I could unravel my thoughts at last. I had come to these stairs thinking I could be restored somehow by this stranger, that Faith Hale could save me from the dark states, my father's voice calling me into death, but it seemed a gamble in which the stakes were so excruciatingly high I would do better falling asleep right here, lying on this step, with my drenched being under the chandelier, until morning broke.

"Hey, who's here?" The voice from the left wing sounded slightly hoarse, but it was insistent and strong, and it had broken through the dim lighting. "What happened? It's Faith, is this Lizzie?"

I reached for the banister, hoisting myself up.

"Wait a minute; come on you fucker, come on." The woman started slapping at the light switch on the wall, her enormous head of hair wound into a top-bun with a braid circumscribing it. Her face became clearer in the warm spot of light from the chandelier. Faith was wearing a plain forest green turtleneck and denim skirt and bright red, scuffed Keds sneakers. "I can't see a god-damn thing," she said. "Why can't they get some decent lighting in here? What's a matter with these people? It's lousy. You see they use these fancy buildings for classes, maybe to impress the rich donors, then they don't fix them up to have normal lights. And the bathrooms are terrible. Who can use them? What a bunch of bums. Lizzie, is that you there?"

"No, my name is Allegra."

"Oh." Faith said. "I thought you were that kid, Lizzie. She hangs around a lot."

"I was just resting; I have to go back to my dorm in Garrison, down the hill. I'm sorry."

"For what?" Faith asked.

"I was just trying to rest."

"Come on, it's cold as hell outside. For Chrissakes, don't go back out in it. You're probably soaked. I think I have an afghan in my office." Faith paused. "You are soaked," Faith said as she drew close. "That can cause health complications. Come to my office. It's just to the left of here. They gave me a small office, but I don't take such things personally."

The chandelier light poured down on me as I had started to shiver.

"You look scared," Faith said. "Friendly as you are, and not to mention a good-looking girl, you seem like you're scared of something. I'm scared of a lot of things, so don't take my inquiry wrong."

"I'm not—"

"Wait! I have to cough," Faith suddenly said. Then she balanced herself against me, her right hand clutching my shoulder as she leaned into me, bowing. "OK, here it comes." Two, three coughs exploded as she cupped her mouth with her free hand. "Wait, maybe there's more, darling." Then she finally let go of me. "I always have to hold onto someone when I cough, it's not explainable."

I felt an involuntary laugh uproot my anxiety. I felt I'd been enfolded into Faith's great performance, my distress taken away too.

"Yeah, it's funny, OK," Faith said, "but look, I want to tell you I had a friend who stayed out in the rain too long and she got instantaneous pneumonia. I personally never heard of instantaneous pneumonia before my friend explained to me its destructive travel down her esophagus and its true condition. She may have died if not for a friend pulling her inside from the rain to a warm living room. Now I'm worried about that kid Lizzie. I thought I would see her again tonight."

I followed Faith through opened double doors into the vast emptiness of a classroom. A wooden table stood in the center, an antique mahogany with scratching etched into its shellac surface; there was a fireplace with engraved columns and an entablature. Faith was still talking about the lighting and the bathroom, loudly, as if some lurking but unseen authority might hear her protest.

"Just one fucking decent light bulb, and one normal toilet, you rotten bums, for the ladies who don't have the equipment to stand so long during nature's call. Wait a minute," Faith said as we walked through a small kitchen to her office door. Soon we entered the cluttered office space and Faith went to get a hand-crocheted afghan from its windowsill. Faith unfurled it and spread it across my shoulders, and I smelled something clean and damp, as if wet leaves had blown in. Faith had left the window open just a slender inch. I couldn't disconnect these natural fragrances from the short, tender woman with those huge eyes. Or the broad cheekbones and nest of bunned hair above long, wild, uncombed strands. Faith was not comic in demeanor, but looked serious, which made her confusing to me. There was a certain gravity in Faith's face, as if she were on the verge of telling me or everyone something monumentally important. Perhaps, I suddenly thought, Faith, like me, felt at fault for something: that something had to be fixed.

I kept quiet and still. Faith's stuffed office was full of dog-eared paperbacks, half-drunk cups of herbal teas, and tangerines, the peels piled on a lovely China plate.

"You have to be cockeyed to go out in the rain like you did," Faith said. "I've been in my office most of the night, working. I have this thing I must go over." On Faith's desk, I spotted a stack of what looked like political pamphlets with peace signs on them, crudely and simply printed in blurry black and white, and a map copied from a magic marker original. It was clear Faith had been folding them; half a pile was done and lay separated near her black telephone. "Listen, a friend just gave me some vitamin B pills, so you're lucky tonight. I have a whole bottle in my office. You'll live, darling, after you have the vitamin B and maybe some orange juice. They're good for things like this happening to a person."

"This is very kind."

"Oh, not really," Faith said. "I mean, this is what a person does. For another person, I mean. It's natural."

I was still shivering, though I was under the afghan now. Then I felt a sudden flow of warmth in the small office. I had to think fast; why was I here? Faith would soon ask. I could lie and say I needed to tell someone on the writing faculty about Dickers and Susan Hunt. How could I say it was about Dickers's reaction to my manuscript? Would I have to tell Faith that I'd brought my pages to Dickers with huge desire, and that this encounter was soon followed by hearing Susan Hunt tell me she had slept with Dickers at the Howard Johnson motel? Susan Hunt, I thought. . . who flaunted her body and breasts before me as if she and Dickers were in collusion somehow, expecting me to take my seat as their spectator and audience, to even feel honored to do so, offering me the whole front row—a forced looking which crushed all the acts of being I had pulled out of myself that summer to write the pages that were now stuffed inside the Hefty bag.

Suddenly, Faith's earnest stare began to shame me, as if the same brown eyes that could be so soft could also be hard enough to question whether I might be upset about absolutely nothing at all, a little disturbance that would make me feel like a child complaining about a splinter in her foot. It seemed a risk to say anything more, so I remained still.

"What is it?" Faith asked. "You look like a little monk sitting there. Should we pray or something?"

I became confused by the ongoing rush of warmth flowing in my body, which I was sure did not come from the afghan alone, but from something deeper. A series of giggles spread inside my throat as I laughed. Something passed through my system, like a relief, a release. . .a cure?

"Yeah," Faith said as if I really had just confessed something essential by finally laughing at myself and my own intensity. Faith pulled out the chair from her desk and leaned back into it, placing her hands behind her head and waiting intensely for me to speak again. She started stretching, her arms spreading out. "Tell me," she said. "What's up with you, sister?"

But just as Faith focused on me, I, in contrast, struggled to find focus at all, and when I didn't say anything, Faith leaned forward. "What's in the garbage bag you're hanging onto there, Toots?" she asked, her elbows on her knees, her eyes growing larger.

"I saw M.B. Dickers," I said quickly.

"Oh, him, yeah, OK. A big shot." Faith said.

"Dickers didn't think it was any good."

"What wasn't any good, darling?"

"My novel. It's in the garbage bag. He is so famous, you know."

"Yeah. I heard."

"Well, actually, I came here to tell you about my friend and Dickers." I hesitated, not wanting to go into the humiliation with Dickers or, later, with Susan Hunt. And wondering, too, why I felt the sudden need and urge to betray Susan Hunt.

"Oh."

"People said you would care and so I wanted to tell you, Mrs. Hale. Dickers is with my friend."

"Call me Faith, first of all,"

"Faith."

"Why're you worried about your friend?"

"Because M.B. Dickers. . . she's going to meet him in a motel room again."

"Oh, yeah, I get the idea."

"I wanted—I needed to tell someone on the writing faculty. It felt important."

"I can see you are a very good person. I saw that immediately," Faith said. I feel foolish, I wanted to say, wrapped in the seductive warmth of Faith Hale. My right hand slid down my wet jeans and seemed to be moving involuntarily, as if to scrape off the damp from the downpour.

"Anyway, darling," Faith continued, "I don't require an explanation. I see that you have troubles. I want you to stay here until you feel good enough again to go back to your room. I'll put a 'Do Not Disturb' sign on the door, like in one of those hotels, what do you call them. The hotels, not the sign, I mean."

Faith's mind was full of associations, flights that made sudden surprising connections and improbable sense, I was learning. As Faith talked, I thought: I will leave intact. How strange a condition I had, the ominous states always threatening me, myself always despairing me. I wanted to tell Faith about the dark states and the virus, but I stayed still and listened.

"M.B. Dickers is part of your education, bastard that he is," Faith continued. "I'm not saying he isn't an ass." She paused, then added: "But for instance, if you're going bald and fat, and then you write a book and get famous, you're suddenly a big shot who can get women, whereas before you were just a dope." Now Faith's eyes pointed themselves at the green Hefty bag again, its weighty cargo — my pages.

"Let me take a look at your writing inside that garbage bag, will you?" Faith said after a pause. "I won't tell a soul about what you told me of your friend and Dickers. Maybe you want to not stay here but go back to your dormitory room now that you're calmer. I'll keep your pages safe with me tonight. Maybe you can come back, say in a day or so, or better, tomorrow morning, and we can talk about your pages. I'll have them read by then."

I nodded weakly but with excitement.

"I want you to get a notebook. No, wait, I think I have one." Faith's fingers rummaged through a stack of student's work and pulled from underneath it a student's plain notebook with a spiral wire binding. It could have been where some student of biology recorded their class notes, I thought. "Take this," Faith said to me. "Someone left it here and I looked inside. It's bare. Fill it with the poetry or prose of your heart beating, of yourself, and your notes on living. That's writing, too."

I brought the notebook to myself, carefully.

Faith went into the small kitchen while I finally pulled my pages out of the Hefty bag to rest on my crossed legs. I heard Faith swearing now at the tea kettle and the gas stove. Then I saw Faith's handwriting for the first time on a few scattered postcards and lined paper that had drifted down onto the floor in the chaos of Faith's activities. There it was in pencil — Faith's beautifully crafted, controlled strokes — loops and circles and perfect stems and slanted letters, so unlike Faith herself.

Faith came back with a bag of rusks, a glass of orange juice, a cup of tea, and two B vitamins on a saucer. She placed them all on the floor near me, then said loudly, "I wish I had cheese." She went back into the kitchen and returned holding a teacup with steaming herbal tea and orange juice on a saucer, which she now piled with rusks. "It seems right that you told me this about M.B. Dickers and your friend. You were looking out for her, Cookie," Faith said, bringing her own cup of tea and a few rusks to her desk, then sitting in her wooden desk chair. "I feel like we can talk for maybe forty years about all the reasons Dickers is what he is and feels so entitled to everything," Faith said. "It must feel like a great absence in yourself, that he dismissed your important writing, if that's what's bugging you, darling. So come into my class. I'll talk to What's-Her-Name in the dean's office. Some bad things have happened in my life too."

I took down the B vitamins with sips of tea and nibbled on some of my own rusks as Faith sipped her herbal tea. Faith's bites and chewing were loud.Faith did not clean off the wet particles of rusk and tea that settled on her chin, and the pleasure of her noisy joy — Faith's unabashed appetite — made my face flush. Surely this would all be analyzable later in my dormitory room when I mulled over what may have occurred just in the moments between entering the soft, messy room and sitting myself down like this, the cup of tea in my warming hands. And the waves of sudden well-being occupying my distraught nervous system, as I watched Faith ready to tell a story with a joke. Faith Hale, I thought, was the possibility of human kindness. It was of Faith I might one day say something insufficient and embarrassing like "I never met anyone like her," because I had no other words.

I kept still. I sipped more of my orange juice and took some of the rusks, which tasted sweet and crumbly, from the saucer on the floor. Suddenly, Faith jumped out of her seat, exclaiming, "Wait, there's strawberry jam! I swear I saw it in the kitchen!" Faith hurried back into the kitchen and I heard her opening and slamming cupboard doors.

"What? You took your writing out of the bag, OK, give me a page, I want to see," Faith said as she came back into the room, empty-handed. I was courageously holding my pages now. "I'm an okay person, you know. And I see how you're suffering. I mean only good. Also, there is no strawberry jam. I need to announce this just in case, like me, you were expecting something more with these rusks. These are the true crises in a person's life, running out of jam and such."

A laugh came again, but I held it inside my throat, as pleasure and warmth began rising faster, I found myself handing over my pages to Faith as she bent down, her breasts close to me.

When Faith went back to her desk chair and put the pages on her lap, smoothing them with the flat of her hand, the motion made me feel like I was sinking down into the rug. I was shivering again. I pulled the afghan back over my shoulders, but I wasn't cold, just frightened. I was twisting in the air. The atmosphere was ripe with implication between Faith's enthusiastic whispers of "yeah," "this is very interesting," and "a friend of mine — a good friend — had an abortion," which soon were washing away the dismissal by Dickers and Susan Hunt and the whole nightmare, as if it were something I had only dreamed.

Finally, Faith put down the pages and said: "I'll keep them safe with me here, so come back to me tomorrow morning. I'll be here and have more time to give them. OK, Toots? I'll keep them here with me until then. I like what you're doing here with these pages, bringing us the important news about your life, which is quite interesting, I think. Let me talk to What's-Her-Name, you know — that person in the dean's office, about you coming into my class." Then Faith added: "These Hefty bags are amazing, by the way — they didn't have such things when I was a girl, just brown paper bags, which were no good in the rain, in circumstances such as these. So you see, sweetheart, as much injustice and horror as there is in the world, there are things that are useful."

I watched Faith place my pages carefully over her sundry mess of pamphlets and note pages.

"I am so eager to read more and talk to you about this," Faith said, opening the door to protectively usher me back into the rainy night.

I believed Faith would help me with the dark states, and I felt surging moments of joy as I walked back to my dorm. The sudden and frequent descents into darkness could all be over with Faith's help. Hope was a chord playing in my heart as I grew more excited about Faith reading my novel. I would tell her about them, and about the dark states that descended.

I had walked along the Bronx River many times alone in the evenings before meeting Faith, skipping dinner at Bates. The Bronx River seemed a refuge where the chaos and confusion of the campus and my own emotions could be stilled. The trees towered over it; the darkness and the river water both frightened and compelled me.

I had thought of the people before me who had looked down at the river and maybe, I thought, some had decided to go to sleep forever beneath it like my father had in the sea. Maybe they felt they would never be good enough at anything, too. I also wondered how they had done it — the physical act of suicide. If it was because of the dark states, too, that led them into a final supreme schizophrenia. The day before by the river, I had started thinking about "the Leatherman", the Pound Ridge legend from the late 1800's who was said to be a mysterious French hermit, roaming eastern Westchester County for nearly thirty years. Dressed in a patchwork leather suit, he followed a regular circuit of approximately 350 miles every 34 days, in his leather shoes and belt, sleeping in caves and taking meals at friendly farmhouses. His shoes were even leather patches sewn together. No one seemed to know what kind of madness or peaceful insanity he, the Leatherman, fostered in his mute person, roaming around like that, nor did anyone ever say he was dangerous. But even the thought of his ghost — the story of which made all the girls writhe at a slumber party when I was young (and some even screamed as Marianne Wheeler continued to tell them he was about to crash our schoolgirl gathering), who many thought was a ghost of a "crazy" man, was more feared than the wild horses on Fancher Road, even more than the copperheads in the forests, and more than the spirits of the first inhabitants of the land, the Siwanoy and Kitchawong, Indians of the Mohican tribes whose tomahawks could still be found in the Pound Ridge woods.

I tried to remember what they had all done to protect themselves against this vagrant, harmless, mentally ill man. And in the silence of the evening by the river, I wondered about all the mad and the dead — the suicides — because their days had ended and I did not quite know how I would get through mine. Would I be like the Leatherman if the dark states didn't stop? Would I be like my father and join him in death? In writing, my internal life could be an epic with a drama at its center, just like some adventure in which I was trying to escape an inflamed and evil virus, a devil, or a gun.

I had sometimes seen my father in the river water as if he were calling to me to join him, a quiet and fatal tug. My father returned to inhabit me when I had the dark states. And after the abortion, he seemed to come more frequently, but only in unexpectant spurts of memory, and then my despair and dark states would embrace me like an old returning lover. How I had tried and tried to extinguish them and gotten nowhere. It would be different now, I told myself that night after seeing Faith Hale. Different because I met Faith Hale. I thought of the big Hefty bag of my own birth parts. I had been so certain I would have to abort them too, but feeling Faith near and thinking of tomorrow when Faith had read my novel, my own birth parts would consume me again. In writing were places that did not deceive like the moments in ordinary life. Writing gifted the author — and the reader — with scenes which told of a journey unspeakable to anyone in any other way; it gave blood and breath to what could not be grasped in mere living. Writing would give me a noble rebirth, I thought, embarrassed with a feeling of girlish exuberance. And it would be Faith who helped me have these second limbs and heartbeats. Which were going to live after all. Now I could sleep. If the darkness came suddenly, as it sometimes did, I would jump up out of bed and write some more pages.

Chapter Three.

Faith Hale had told me to wait only that night to give her time to read and then she had said to come back in the morning, and here it was now. Morning. I couldn't wait to hear what Faith would say. I was so full of hope and nervousness as I walked up the steep hill to Faith's office after my large breakfast, clutching the notebook Faith gave me, still crazily excited by the promise Faith had made me the night before.

Reaching Andrews, which shone in the morning light, I hurried through the classroom, past the fireplace, to Faith's office. As I approached the office, I slowed down, trying not to appear too eager.

There was a notice taped to the closed door:

> Faith Hale has gone to Chile to protest
> human rights violations. All classes and
> conferences are canceled and will resume
> in two weeks.

I stood, frozen, until I felt my hand touch the paper, the impulse to tear it off the door making it move as if by itself. Then, startled by my anger, and dazed, I retreated to a flagstone portico behind Andrews. I could not return to campus this shaken, I thought. The sun made the green grass look sickly, like it would soon die, like it was almost dead already.

I had been so upset by Faith's note that I stayed in my room and skipped my psychology class that afternoon. I stashed the notebook Faith gave me in my underwear drawer, under my panties, bras, and socks. I did not go to my modern fiction class that afternoon, either. I went to the candy machine and, drawing out three packs of Reese's Peanut Butter Cups and a Hershey's Krackel, I let myself stay under my bedsheets to eat, dwelling in a feverish lull. The room was stale and dirty, its cheap floor made of what seemed like plastic tiles, and the bed a thin mattress inside the metal-framed institutional structure like what I imagined kids waiting for foster homes might sleep on in a halfway house. I smelled the failed morning on myself, not so much perspiration and dirtiness but an unfleshy scent, as if I had been rubbed in dust and debris. I smelled of the vanished night, a rainy night that had meant so much to me, Faith Hale and her sunshine of cure then a possibility.

I had no immediate plan but to find the desire to get out of the bed. My pages were in someone else's hands. I wondered if my father would come back now, if I'd hear his voice and see him again in my mind beckoning me to him in another world that was death. Faith was gone, and all my pages were in her office, so they were all gone, too, I thought. I wasn't thinking clearly when I reached for the phone in my dorm room and called my mother, the only person I knew who would be there.

"So," Sofia, my mother, said into the phone. "How is it there? Uh-hem?"

"Great," I said, staring at my bitten fingernails.

"Oh, so great," Sofia mimicked. "'Great', really?"

"You know what I mean, Mami. Nothing to complain about so far. It's still too early." Sofia is chapter one, I suddenly thought, Sofia is chapter one of the novel still in the garbage bag. My mind drifted now to avoid both my mother's tone and what my mother might say next.

"I suppose I should send you some more money," Sofia said. "Are you there, Allegra? Did we get cut off?"

Faith would have found chapter one, I thought, if she hadn't deserted. "No, Mami," I said. "It's not necessary to send more money, I'm fine."

"Well, as for me," Sofia started, "I write my poems first thing when I get up, it's still nearly dawn, and I have my tea and Familia muesli. I sit by the wide window, and I can see the birds from the forest helping themselves to the seeds I laid for them. The stillness makes life simple." Clichés never really sounded like clichés when Sofia spoke them. For all her callous disregard for others, Sofia was so self-possessed and unassailable, her descriptions of her morning meditations written in her hand-bound, silk-covered notebooks were mysteriously lavish and fresh-sounding. I remembered that birdhouse, my mother's crafted birdhouse, perfectly laid with wooden roof and sides, a metal net as its gate and inside it were seeds and a tiny water trough. Sofia woke very early most mornings and went down to her country kitchen, brewed her tea, ate her muesli with skim milk and perfectly carved half bananas, then cleared the curtain that fell over the wide kitchen window to observe what bird might have fed in her carefully crafted birdhouse. She had started the birdhouse after throwing away my father's books. She said she could never understand books by Proust and others in the library like them that made her feel "stupid;" she had thrown the books out, in a rage, wild-eyed. My mother only had a high school education, and even that she never finished for a high school degree.

Sofia's own father in Argentina had become wealthy in the Argentinean cattle business, and now Sofia, independently rich, could immerse herself in her dance and her dance recitals, and her "poetry" which she wrote even before my father, Edward, died. She had built a dance studio, and her Isadora Duncanesque free spirit dance recitals in the Bedford Church drew in crowds of bell-bottomed admirers. Her lean, exotic looks graced rooms and stages. She became increasingly exotic. In the "new life" (after Edward's death), Sofia was "cool," self-possessed; her imperfect features — long, curved nose and tight mouth — translated into a beautiful, soulful older woman with an "interesting" face. Sofia and I would sit on the red couch in the living room, and Sofia talked about her deep loneliness in Argentina as a girl, "What's the matter with you, Allegra? As for me, my mother called me a slut, *la puta*. I would remember this and then I would forget it; I hadn't even let one boy go further than kissing and touching me with my clothes on. It was because I ordered those American stockings from the catalogs and waited to wear them just to get my mother upset." Sofia's dramatic monologues were long and mostly for herself.

"Tell me," Sofia said now on the phone. "Have you found what it is you seek? You have an old soul, Allegra."

There it was, I told myself, some love in my mother's voice, imparting through pure aural suggestion the image of Sofia, the graceful, controlled Sofia, with her black straight hair. Sofia, whom I could never match for pure physical prowess, either finding myself crushed under Sofia, or swaying to the music of Sofia's domination, waiting for the infrequent expressions of maternal love.

"I'm fine, Mami," I had lied. "I started classes. It's going to be fine here. I'm writing."

"Uh-hem. Is it snowing there? Here, it's been raining very much. I wonder if Richard Bach will ever write a sequel to Jonathan Livingston Seagull. That's the kind of writing for me, dear one, I'm sorry. You and your father's —"

"Lots of rain, Mami," I continued, cutting my mother's other words off as fast as I could. "I'm in Bronxville, it's only half an hour away from you, it has the same weather."

"Did you think I didn't know that? I'm not ignorant you know."

Mami, please let's not start, I thought.

"I'm just as intellectual as you," Sofia stated. "I write in my journal. My body is a poem, too."

"Of course it is. But Mami, I met a famous writer here and she loved my book. Her name is Faith Hale." For a reason I didn't understand, I suddenly lied.

I was sure I heard a little gasp from Sofia. "Faith Hale? *The* Faith Hale?" my mother asked. And after I said "yes," Sofia simply didn't say anything else. A silence fell between us. How different it would be if instead of having to listen to Sofia's grandiloquent voice that filled the spaces of air in the communication we shared, I could cry and break down and tell my mother how frightened I was here, that it wasn't true — I had just made that part about Faith Hale up; it was all a fantasy. Faith had really deserted me after only one conference on a rainy night. If only my mother had some spare place in her heart for my voice. Here I was in this whorehouse of performers, Abigail Stone College, and why couldn't my mother be different? And there Sofia was in the beautiful Pound Ridge colonial house with

all her Argentinean furniture, the hand-painted bureaus
and a chest in the hallway, free of my father's books
which made her once feel so looked down upon and
shut out of his life, in the square living room with glass
doors, looking out onto a forest. Sofia had developed the
bird feeding schedule that previous summer when I was
home, and now I was imagining how the maple autumn
leaves must be filling Sofia's meticulously placed water
bowls for the birds. The sad, lonely and isolated Sofia
and her birds, both flying off into opaque worlds, Sofia
purposefully obfuscating her meanings from others. A
mild depression always wafted through Sofia, as if her
very breathing exhaled it each time she let out a tired,
exasperated sigh at the sight of me. I suddenly remembered her telling me about a Bedford couple who came
to look at some of her rare Argentinean prints and how
Sofia kept saying about the visit, "This couple, they're all
bullshit." I didn't know whether she meant the couple
was all bullshit or the prints, but soon gave up trying
to figure out which. I will make Mami happy, I once
thought. When we disagree, I will tell her she is right,
she knows better than I do. I will say these things so I
will be both supremely nourished by her crumbs of approval and undermined at the same time, and filled in an
agony of resentment. I believed I had given up the struggle to feel love by submission. I thought I had given this
struggle up like that last bottle of Macallan's single malt
scotch which helped me fall asleep in my bedroom in my
mother's house before Sofia drove me to Abigail Stone (I
had promised myself I wouldn't drink at Abigail Stone).
This need to keep wanting to please my mother, to sort
through each comment, as if some drip of approval or
even warmth would exit from Sofia's lips and how good
it would feel when and if it did come, like the warmth of
a sun in an Arctic exile, was more addictive than alcohol.

"Okay, so this conversation is over, I think," Sofia said now, suddenly. "It doesn't feel like you need me much. . .there."

"Mami, please. I do."

"Well, I've been reordering the house a bit. You know, in my way. I'm thinking of tossing some more of those old books on your father's bookshelf. I want to convert his library into an extra guest room."

I swallowed. They had souls, these discarded books, I thought, and presences like breathing objects. I couldn't bear any thought of their demise under her hands. "I'll take them, Mami. I will," I said.

"I am glad you are there, Allegra," my mother said, as if she hadn't heard my words. "We all go through life in cycles and find ourselves at crossroads we can't at first decipher. I, of course, have suffered a lot. Cape Elizabeth, that long-ago sadness after your father did what he did. . .you know it has taken its toll, and I am now beginning to find the spaces that I gave away, filling them again with my dreams, and my own search for answers. This is a difficult and wonderful time of our lives, don't you see? But with that said, I must say that I was not prepared for my sixties!"

"Oh, Mami, you look beautiful!"

"So yes, I am fine and no, I am not fine. This is the paradox that in a magic way keeps me vital. It is not a negative, but simply the way it has been. . .the challenge is to find something new and healing within the sameness of our longings and pain."

"I hope we can lunch here," I said. "They have a very good restaurant in the village."

"We'll see." Sofia said.

"Yeah," I said.

"Uh-hem. . .goodbye, Allegra. Goodbye, little sweetheart, we are in a new era, think of it as a new age for all of us. Your brother, Julian, too. We three, entering autumn's dark lights and winter's foreboding to become ourselves, each apart and growing, but not really growing apart."

"I'll try to do that, Mami." I said.

"It's strange how we have all grown, if you think about it. I ponder it often." Sofia said. Then there she was again. The seductive, beautiful Sofia I loved for all her statuesque weirdness, who preferred decorating hallways to actual rooms. And was as seductive as she was organized and "perfect." In her decorated hallways, she could stand with the rustic antique hall mirrors and bureaus observing her guests in the living room, a superior distance from others. She made me appear, in contrast, messy and slightly out of control. "You have an old soul," Sofia had often told me. "But you're a little girl. You know I believe we have had other lives before this. I'm an old soul as well. I personally am looking for self-transcendence, the unknowing cloud that brings perfect expressiveness. This perhaps is the paradox we all must face, Allegra, so we aren't phonies." Sofia shared her ponderances, then quickly said, "Well, okay. Bye, dear daughter."

"Bye."

Feeling cold after I hung up the phone, I picked up my scratchy grey army blanket, wondering why it had fallen to the floor as I was speaking to Sofia. An ant was crawling on its thin wool. I plucked it up, held it between my two fingers, and crushed it. I had killed this hardly visible ant only with the pinch of my forefinger and thumb. I was staring at its dots of remains, ashamed at how good the killing had felt, wondering what was wrong with me that I had relished killing it. The dark, Gothic ambience of Abigail Stone College must have seeped into me. There were more ants in my room — I was sure. I was glad for the phone in my own room.

Sofia had sent the check for the installation. I was glad, too, that my dorm room door had been closed and no one in the dormitory or hall could overhear our conversation. From Sofia, I could endure any amount of loneliness and humiliation; I was a bottomless well: here I am — I am a well, I am the well of the failed, the pathetic, the childish, the embarrassing, the messy, and over-dramatic. The well of the one who should have drowned in the sea instead of him. I deserve chastisement. I will endure. It excites me to endure you, Mother.

But my mind was drifting, and for some reason I didn't understand, I was remembering how I had lain supine on the gynecologist's cot after the abortion. My thoughts were falling more and more under the spell of Faith's, which alarmed and frightened me, but then the spell was helping phase out the fingers and speculum which had first probed into my uterus that day in the abortion clinic, and then into the horror of that which I had to kill and lose, created within me by a night's mistake — how it was slowly, sterilely removed, inch by inch, by the abortion doctor.

I remembered getting an IUD inserted into my womb after the mass was taken from me — still flat on my back, my feet inside steel stirrups fixed from the end of the cot. With the speculum holding my vagina open, the doctor had swabbed my vagina and cervix with antiseptic solution and inserted the tenaculum, an instrument that went through to my cervix. He pushed it in and it made a uterine sound, and I had wondered if my uterus played music and, if so, could I hear it, too? What was my flesh playing? Then soon there had been overwhelming pain, the cramps overcame me as if vaginal waves were mutilating my sex, as if I had been punched in my clitoris, and I felt uncanny reverberations throughout my womb. The doctor pushed a tube through the tenaculum to my cervix which I thought must have held the IUD, pulled the tube back to release the arms of the IUD, and pushed it to the top of my uterus with the tip of the tenaculum. Finally, the doctor pulled the tenaculum out and made sure the IUD's strings were hanging through my cervix into my vagina, and that the IUD held inside me. For help during the procedure, I looked up at the poster on the wall for the book "Sisterhood Is Powerful". I had seen the real book on Faith's shelf while she was rummaging through the kitchen cupboards for strawberry jam, the beguiling feminist symbol on its red cover which looked like a communist hammer and sickle, or insignia for one of those illegal underground lesbian clubs in the West Village. The spell of that poster and Faith's warmth was in my thoughts, which alarmed and frightened me, and then the spell was helping phase out the memory of my mother, E.M. Dickers and Susan Hunt, and even the abortion.

Yes, Faith must come back, I told myself. I could hope. I got up and showered, putting expensive conditioner in my hair after I washed it.

The bottle said, "the art and science of pure flower and plant essences."

Faith would still save me from the dark states.

Something new was happening now that I had met Faith Hale. I was glad I hadn't taken the mirror from my old bedroom in Bedford. I was going to come into being from a different point than my mother's distant heart.

I was filled now with an unfamiliar excited, hopeful feeling because I believed that Faith would be back and would read my novel, that she might be even reading it in her West Village apartment. It was true that my first novel didn't have three acts or an outside plot, but inside me, a story, a journey still lay I knew; anyway did Faith Hale care about three acts? From what I knew of Faith Hale and her own writing, it was the dark and hidden lives of young women and their yet unwritten lives she sought to support. I had read about her in the newspapers and in the Abigail Stone College description of professors and visiting artists. But my novel of "a young woman" was a written mess of events, characters, and emotional landscapes, haphazard as a throw of dice. An unrestrained, stormy collage of images and memories. I wrote about the horror of the dark states and how my father was calling me sometimes in a soft seduction to death. There were pages about Sofia, "once a member of the first Argentinean dance troupe in Buenos Aires" I wrote. Sofia had a pompadour hairdo in the pictures of her as a young woman in Buenos Aires, a statuesque, cold woman even back then. I described it this way: "Sofia stared down from a long neck at her daughter, piously and judgmentally." But there were also pages full of descriptions of the apple orchards and waterfalls of Pound Ridge where I lived with my mother and my younger brother Julian for all those years before and after my father's death. My mother was also part of that beauty and bountifulness. Somewhere in the spill of words, I had told of the summer oceanfront house on Cape Elizabeth, off the coast of Maine where, when I was fourteen, my father had walked down the grassy slope and then plunged himself into the Atlantic Ocean, drowning by suicide.

There was a Rilke poem I never forgot. My father gave it to me that same year I turned fourteen. It was a few months before his death:

How shall I hold my soul so it does not
touch on yours?
How shall I lift it over you to other
things?
Ah, willingly I'd store it away with some
lost thing in the dark—
O sweet Song.

That winter after my father's death in 1967, Sofia
went with me and Julian to close up the summerhouse,
that beautiful cottage close to an old lighthouse and
sand dunes so enormous to me as a child they looked
like mountains. The winter sun was dim and pale as
a boiled onion; there was barely any light even in the
house except for my father's two antique lamplights,
which had to be lit to see the rooms. In the white light
outside, I had seen my father present again as an image,
standing strongly on the rocks in the sea wind as he had
been before he drowned. It felt like just yesterday. He
was in his blue swimsuit, shirtless, his square, perfectly
crested chest with its silken hair open to the sea breeze,
standing with legs like a long distance runner still in
his youth. In my memory, he was perched imperially
between two crags. I wanted to get to him, but there was
a wide crevasse I needed to cross. His outstretched arm
was beckoning me to hop between one crag and another
like he did when he was alive. "Come on," he was saying
again softly in my imagination. "Well, come on. You can
make it, Allegra."

The father I had lost was mercurial in my memories.
I kept losing him as he deconstructed into clues and
pieces about who he was and who he might have been.
I tried to hold onto him. But when I remembered him
sitting in his room alone in the dark, as if in mourning

some days, in the grip of his frequent depressions and feelings of being a failure in this life, I wondered if I had inherited the dark states from him. I sometimes wanted to put him and my memories away entirely. And to forget the summers of family happiness on Cape Elizabeth before 1967 — the family summer cottage and previous life filed in my subconscious under a category I called the "other life." It was far too painful to recall because of the ache it elicited and the light it threw on my present life.

When I met my father downstairs for breakfasts that he prepared for us in that "other life," he was usually in his undershirt and slacks and barefoot, and he pulled the chair behind him to sit closer to the table. I remembered the heat of the eggs on the plate; they were like two eyes watching us. I remembered oily kippers on the plate, fishy cuts, salty and erotic. I remembered Maine fogs and Maine rainfalls and Maine seas. I also remembered that he looked diminished in the bed he had shared with Sofia in the cold Maine nights when I walked in to kiss him goodnight. And what had excited me was how small I was in comparison to my mother. Sofia was always taller than my father, and that discrepancy seemed to upset the balance of the universe as well as my personal sense of things. I wanted it this way, me very small, very much the follower of my father's clean, soft footfalls on the wooden floors of the Maine cottage and on the beach.

When I was eleven, he sat on the swing chair outside on the lawn. I stood, he brought me to him; I wasn't sure I remembered it the way it was, his fresh evening scent on me, his clean square-nailed hands holding me between his legs which were spread, how I sensed the closeness of his penis. I knew only the animated way he spoke to me then, as if I had brought him out of a cold tomb, with my little body which I wanted to be little and had no problem being little, right between his legs, and then Sofia walking out to us.

He loves me more than you, Mother, I had thought then. I am little and you are too tall. Too dominating and cold. I am his because I am little. Sofia was stately and impressive, but not beautiful. But that was not Sofia's fault, I told myself often, still not wanting to hurt this mother whose efficiency and control was as vital to me as my father's expansive dreaminess. What I loved in the "other life" was that Sofia was different, my mother could be warmer toward me then, and when Sofia was cold at other times, there had been enough warmth from my father to change the temperature in the air.

"Your father had a great unhappiness, Allegra. He was not a strong man." Sophia said that winter. After he had disappeared, I could not forget how the police searched the sea, their big, black rubber boots on. My father had washed up finally, a mile down the beach and after the police came to our door, my mother — self-possessed, cold as the Cape Elizabeth night — told me I couldn't come with her to the village morgue to identify the body; I was "too young" and I shouldn't remember my father "that way." I watched the white glimmers from the night sea out the kitchen window in the night; the kitchen was cloaked in darkness. I took out a splitting knife meant for lobster — my father's favorite was Maine lobster — envisioned the silken butter, my father at the kitchen table, cracking a lobster claw, his soft eyes. . .but with this knife I had deliberately carved into my thigh until blood beaded and rose, a line of fascinating bubbles. I let out a gasp, but continued to slit into my thigh, the blood streamed as if an intruder, someone outside myself was doing it, carrying out the brutal act. I put a dishtowel over my thigh and thought maybe someday I would understand why I did this. I thought I might know already, that I wanted to be with my father if it was only for a few seconds of painful sensations. But then my mother, disciplined, distanced, meticulous, appeared before me:

"Why?" Sofia asked, but without much emotion. Sofia flicked on the bright fluorescent light, quickly tightened the dishtowel around the bleeding, and then had thrust me into the backseat of her Jaguar with Julian. While driving me to the emergency room, the blood still seeping from my thigh, Sofia repeatedly shook her head with expressionless eyes.

Sofia took me to the Maine County hospital with Julian holding the wrapped towel tightly around my bleeding thigh in the backseat of the car. Julian whispered to me, "it's all right, we're at the emergency room, it's going to be fine." Then came an injection from a long hypodermic needle. And then a drowsiness. Julian was still beside me and Sofia was nowhere to be seen. I had needed eight stitches, two in the thigh muscle and six in the skin overlying the muscle. Sofia barely said a word the whole time in the hospital and kept putting small wads of Kleenex with her free right hand under my thigh as we drove back to the cottage, in case blood dripped onto the car seat. That night and the next morning, there was a painful swelling under the bandage. And it was my brother, Julian, who had stayed in my bedroom with me, bringing me Oreo cookies and cold milk, sleeping in an armchair beside my bed, with Sofia coming in and out, brisk and efficient. In the "new life," I became the dark, messy daughter of Sofia, "my own enemy" who "liked to make things difficult and very dramatic" (according to Sofia). At other times, Sofia looked at me with a condescension that absorbed her attitude that I was fragile.

"You're in one of those moods like your father's," Sofia would say if I complained about anything at all, no matter how valid my complaint might be — the school-bus being too late on a freezing winter day where I had to brave and bear the cold waiting for it, my bedroom window being too old to close completely, or simply that I saw a mole in the grassy knoll beside the rock garden. I had lost something with Sofia once I had tried to hurt myself. Sofia approached me the way one might a mental patient, or a slightly cracked egg, with doubt and great distrust.

And my father haunted me after he died. He came out of the floorboards in the Pound Ridge house, the colonial bow windows, and my bedroom curtains. The house seemed to throb with loss. Many more than a few times, I felt that fatal tug, my father beckoning, calling on me to join him in death.

After my father died, I went to a forest of ghosts, and in that forest where I used to walk past the craggy apple tree near the swimming pool and then into the woods filled with birch trees and bushes with poisonous red berries. I felt a quiet that was all my own, as I once had in my father's library with his books. Often, I returned to my room after some hours reading or writing about the trees or the Mohican Indians of my imagination and heard my mother downstairs, instructing the maid on how to clean the living room or other rooms. I let the pull to the apple tree and woods loosen as a great wind died down with only a memory of being swept away in-side it. I wanted to exist in the leaves of that old apple tree, remembering its huge bark as an anchor to the liv-ing world inside my father's library and my own words. I couldn't enter his library again as when, before he died, he unlocked the door with a key the size of a shoe and his finger crossed over his lips. "Shush," he would say. And it wasn't because what was inside it was anything alarming or even unique but that it was magical. There was only an egg-white fluffy square rug over the bare wooden floorboards. Six or seven shelves of meticulously dusted old books, some first editions, but most importantly, a Proust trilogy bound in rich Brazilian leather, from a friend or a client I didn't know. And a yellow, lined notepad on his desk from where he had once promised he would tell me, and its pages, the story of his own life, a middle-class son of Russian immigrants, his father a real estate owner in White Plains.

But my father's yellow pad was always empty. After he died, it was as if one could feel the tears from his eyes on its unused pages. He shined and kept up his five-hundred-dollar Sheaffer fountain pen more than he ever wrote in that yellow pad. My mother locked the door to his library after he died. She now slept alone, without the haunting ruin of this man I barely knew, but who had the keys to some magical kingdom of books, and writing pads, and Marcel Proust.

Why wasn't me loving my father enough for my father, I thought. Why couldn't he ever write his own life? I had failed him somewhere deep and certain. Somewhere absolute, I was certain.

Chapter Four.

A few days after the evening I spoke to Sofia on the
phone, I sat on the chair outside M.B. Dickers's office. It was morning. I had been forced back to Dickers,
terrified of losing college credit if I didn't attend. Plus,
Faith still wasn't back to rescue me. I thought about
telling him: "I saw Faith Hale and she loved my pages"
but I was scared; he then might find out I told on him
about the motel and Susan Hunt. I had eked out three
pages of a brand new "novel" — something about a middle-class college girl at an elite Eastern women's college
bombing buildings in New York City — but I hadn't
fleshed it out yet. It was based on the true Jane Alpert
story, a real young woman who was arrested in 1970 for
participating in the bombing of eight buildings in New
York. I thought if I was "political" and wrote something
against the Vietnam War as all Dickers's writing was, I
could, at the same time, hang on until Faith returned.
The realities of the times I was living through broke
through my haze as when a stray and mangy cat from
the New York streets once wandered onto the perfect
cardboard set of *The Edge of Night* where I had a bit part
as an actress at last, after doing so many walk-ons. The
cat had registered horror amid the stage workers in their
isolated island of recorded, scripted melodramas. It had
taken two stagehands to remove the offending animal,

disappearing out the door with it as if the stench of the poor creature would contaminate them.

In Dickers's own book called *Saul's Lament* he had written things like, "You are a creature of capitalism, the ethics of which are totally corrupt and hypocritical —" and asked questions like, "How can the masses allow themselves to be exploited by the few?" His work had awakened me to the world outside the window of the Pound Ridge hairdresser salon, and set of *The Edge of Night* — a big, violent, and intoxicatingly exciting world quieted slightly by 1973, as the bombings my new novel were based on also were silenced, Jane Alpert jumping bail and disappearing into a mysterious radical underground of women, the "feminists" they were now called.

When Dickers finally opened the door, his office smelled good, like cherry cough drops. I was holding the first pages from my Jane Alpert novel. Dickers stood cordially dressed in a pressed blue suit, and I wondered, could he have taken pains to groom himself for me? His hair was still wet from hair tonic, or was it plain water? I couldn't tell. The office looked massive, and he stood very close to me after he shut the door.

"I see you're really into tobacco," he said as I startled both from his words and the closeness of his body to mine. "The Sherman's," he said, pointing to the pack of special Sherman's Cigarettellos I held on top of my pages which, to my delight, I found I could buy in the college bookstore. "Oh, oh yes." My hands were embarrassing me because I felt them trembling as I gave him my pages. Dickers walked back to his desk; he put on his rimless glasses and sat down. Not looking up again, he motioned to me to take a seat in a large Victorian armchair. As everywhere at Abigail Stone, I never saw a folding chair, or even a plain chair; they were antique cherry wood or Queen Annes, and Dickers's chair was a rich rose mahogany wood. He was a chameleon, I thought, watching him now wave out the huge window at a young male student crossing the grass to a dorm building near the tennis courts. It was almost a cult, his fandom.

"Hey," Dickers said after a few minutes of silence. "This is really kind of mind-blowing that you can change like this. He now had his eyes on my three pages, and when he looked up, I saw that his face was still remote and diffident despite his words; it did not match the clumsy adolescent lingo he liked to try out as real conversation. He tried so hard, I thought, looking at his balding head, his beard, and desert boots. His famous novel, *Saul's Lament*, was about a sixties college student, the son of an electrician in the Bronx who played perfect piano, and frequently had violent coitus with his wife, a plump Jewish woman described in his book as having "androidal prettiness." I had found quotes from his acclaimed novel in an article called "Religion and American Culture" in the library. His novel was about the execution of Sacco and Vanzetti and this young radical named Saul. I had reread eagerly from it two days before, hoping to learn something about writing that might make a person famous someday, and came upon this passage: "Saul gets on top of Nadine's soft, wide ass. . .the brute and torturer, firmly pressing on Nadine's vat of buttery flesh, degrading her sex; she bears his rage at authority, his own marginalization and impotence against it. It doesn't matter when he fucks her but only that he is marginal and powerless in the larger world, only the fucking matters, and her androidal loveliness, her full thighs. Fucking Nadine is how Saul fights back at the world. . ."

I had felt frightened and slightly aroused when I read that passage in my dorm room, and now my eyes were drawn back to Dickers across from me in his office.

"I'm glad to see this. . .uh. . .progress. . .in your three pages." Dickers was saying now. "Allegra. Right, Allegra. . .what nationality is that?"

"I'm from America."

He smiled placidly. "Okay, okay." he said. He didn't look up for those few minutes after, his wide girth on the elegant chair, hands clasped on the right and left edges of my pages.

Dickers thumbed my top page, flicking it rhythmically, fingering a corner.

"I have tried to understand my class, but I must admit I'm having trouble understanding most of the students." Dickers said. He stopped to clear his throat; an old man's noise came out his mouth, not exactly a wheeze, but something equally unpleasant. "I have some worries about the effect of this illegal war. It's a turbulent time for you young people." He might never need me more than at this moment, I suddenly thought; I had qualified in his eyes to bring him at least something useful, something gratifying to his sitting self behind the elegant Abigail Stone desk. "Those girls in your class are obviously all in love with you, Mr. Dickers," I heard myself say, quickly. "They all must have read your novel and fallen in love with you."

His small eyes ignited, twinkled like a dozen hungry stars as he said, "But me? I'm a middle-aged man with some balding up top where you can see. . ." he bowed down his head to me, "and a penchant for Italian pastries." He patted his fattened gut, and his eyes, which when he looked at me, were abruptly vulnerable and a little helpless, looking toward me for strengthening him again, even if it was for only a still, tiny moment.

"No, Mr. Dickers," I said, "Not at all, Mr. Dickers," I said continuing the metaphorical blow job. I swore he let out a great breath of pleasure that made me believe I had, at last, pleased and served him heftily and beautifully so as to relieve him of some great burden. But just as fast other feelings rushed at me.

He leaned back with such satisfaction, the room seemed to heat.

"Yes, Mr. Dickers, of course they're all in love with you," I said watching his face, realizing that I was both innocent and quietly manipulating him. He looked as if I had given him one of the best blow jobs in his life, and even thinking about it, "blow jobs" was proof he had entered my senses. He could have been Sofia, his bearish mass of domination over me, diminishing me at the same time he needed me, and then satiated because of my assuring, admiring, and deceptive words. But all of a sudden, without meaning to or wanting it, I saw myself in my flight of imagination tearing into his cock with my unleashed teeth, a missive from a foreign part of me. If for one minute I could make him feel as small and used as he made me feel, I would delight in that.

"Yes, it is very satisfying to see a student change and grow," he said which made me jolt.

I straightened my back on the chair and stared into Dickers's chubby face.

"Your work is very vigorous," he said, abruptly cutting himself off from me now, either to protect himself or because it was simply time to move on to other things; he had been amply satisfied by me. But now it was clear to me we were done.

Looking out onto the vast campus drive through the window, I yearned to become anonymous and be purged of my own desires to please and murder this man all at once.

The phone rang, and Dickers abruptly dropped my pages on the desktop, standing as he listened to his caller, the fingers of his right hand drumming on my pages.

His face was placid, but he was pulling at his ear lobe. "Thanks, Lou." He finally said, nodding for a reason I didn't know. "Well, what I told him is 'maybe'."

I waited another two minutes for the call to finally end. Dickers looked at me, repressing his fresh new gloating, which obviously now came from the phone call and not me. Then he said, putting the phone receiver back into its cradle, "It was my agent. Did you know they are doing a film about Saul?"

I wanted to respond, but instead I sat perfectly still as he stood and took his blue seersucker jacket up from the back of his chair, pulling his arms alternately through its sleeves, as if he were rushing to go someplace else, his attention no longer on me.

"Well, the movies. . .we writers are like priests," he said in a world-weary arrogance I had never experienced except with Sofia, "preserving the work like old scribes." Dickers cleared his throat. "The class should be helpful to you. And yes, it's good what you wrote," he said, but he was dismissing me.

He was saying things by rote, I thought.

Dickers looked out through the bow window at the tennis courts, put his hands in his pockets, his back to me, and said, as if he had just felt my presence in the room again, "There are many things that make a writer, but you have the main thing. Perseverance." Then, strangely, against my will, I felt a sudden warmth toward him. He changed in that moment, unexpectedly, looking very sad, bereft, cheated. His sweater was too thin, I thought, sympathetically, because it had grown cold outside, now the middle of autumn. I imagined him in rubber boots, emerging from behind his steering wheel with difficulty. He had to be so careful on the roads; it was still his responsibility to drive safely when he had to return to his wife and children. I watched him, too, as I gathered up my pages, looking under the desk as he stood, and I saw how thin his almost hairless legs were compared to his belly and chest. Then, in this drastic changing perspective, he seemed fragile, almost paternal. I wondered whether Susan Hunt, haughty as she seemed to be, thought she was granting a privilege in giving him her body. Did the other girls he had fornicated with at the Howard Johnson Inn have the same attitude? But I only allowed him that charitable sympathy for a few moments, as I imagined him at the Howard Johnson motel after having just fucked another female student who wasn't me.

Then Dickers changed abruptly again. "I've been researching the neutrino," he said, turning around from the window to look at me. "You might want to do that. Just reviewing texts, you know. Scientific texts. Historical texts. Texts. Something completely outside your novel. Consciousness cannot exist without the world, and that isn't very reassuring, is it? Consciousness without the world is nothing at all," he said and then he was off again, I thought, into his masturbatory aloofness and impenetrableness which granted him, I was sure, the real pleasures of his life. "The neutrino is especially fascinating, Allegra," he added after a long pause. "Neutrinos are created as a result of certain types of radioactive decay, or nuclear reactions. Did you know they do not feel the electromagnetic force?"

I shook my head.

"I think the connection to the fact that they have found so many in the atmosphere of late, I mean after Hiroshima, is quite compelling," Dickers continued. "Why all these neutrinos?"

I had smiled because I actually felt warm again toward him as he drifted off into his remote, disconnected thoughts. He turned back to the window.

"There's a feminist here, Faith Hale," he suddenly said. "I don't know if she gets the larger themes. Above women and men, of course. which is so important, as they say."

I did not answer.

"Be careful of feminist rhetoric," he added, "is all I mean."

"Mr. Dickers," I started, clearing my throat with the wetness fear was creating in my throat. "I showed the pages you didn't like to Faith Hale."

"Faith Hale," he said, but his stumbling seemed false. "Yes, well, you could say about her that feminism has found a place these days."

Dickers didn't turn around until he felt me leaving the room, and then he walked to where I was standing by the closed door. Flustered by his closeness. I turned around, and he caught my eyes with his own. His forefinger found the necklace Sofia had once bought for me, a small silver necklace with a topaz stone dangling from its chain. I thought it would make me feel more that I was safe and home in Pound Ridge, as it had reminded me of so many of Sofia's Argentinean necklace stones. He let the chain wrap itself as a coil on his finger while penetrating me with a look into my eyes. "Nice," he said, but he was looking down at my breasts behind my turtleneck sweater. Then all at once, he unspun the necklace chain from his finger and his eyes lowered even further down my body. It felt like my brains were floating inside my head; I was losing my balance. After what felt like seconds, his hand fell from my neckline as if what might be expected under that sweater didn't quite meet his requirements. Disappointment and then a slight impatience to get rid of me from his office seemed to overtake him. His look had only diminished me, painfully. I felt emptied and used but horribly aroused. Had my breasts looked larger to him when he was eyeing them from a distance? I didn't know. I felt my gut sink, then opened the door in a sudden hurry.

"Thank you, Mr. Dickers," I sputtered, as I walked out the door.

That same day, at lunch, Faith Hale walked into the dining hall. There had been decent lunches and dinners in the Bates cafeteria to load up on, expanding my girth. I put my brown plastic tray down on a table where some students had etched graffiti with safety pins for pens: "Abigail Stone is a sell-out dyke factory" and "Can you dig it?" and "Hey, good-looking."

Faith brought the feel of an outside world, an everydayness in her simple clothing and Keds sneakers, especially next to the flamboyant gay student who wore 1920s-style Oxford trousers with billowing legs and red suspenders, now playing a stylish campy version of "The Charleston" at the piano in the center of the room. I watched as Faith sat at the piano next to him after some jostling and joking I hadn't been able to hear. All at once, a group circled the piano and Faith started pounding out Chopin's Études, sliding and slipping on the keys, which didn't embarrass or stop her. She played it anyway, but with dissonance and wrong notes. Every three minutes or so she stopped to correct, sticking out her tongue teasingly, like someone playing a scratched-up record. Then I watched her go around the room after she played. Even as she stood up, students seemed to flock to her. And then, Faith stopped where I was eating, leaned down to my ear and whispered, "I loved your pages. The trip was cut short. Come to my office later, will you Toots? You are a very fine writer, and you know, you're old enough to write a novel, don't you think? And it's important, this novel."

"Mrs. Hale —" I started, barely able to get even those words out.

"I'm Faith," she said. "Call me Faith, darling. Now I feel I must talk to another person in this room of lunchers and luncheons. I'll be in my office at two."

It was one forty-five when I left my dorm room. I had brushed my hair carefully, making sure the mirror showed a calm person even if I was breathing deeply and felt slightly panicked. Faith had not been quite real; what if she would never be real?

There was a cluster of students at Faith's office, waiting for her. Outside her open door, I struggled to get a glimpse of Faith. Finally, through a slight opening, I saw her. Faith was exuberant on her feet, almost dancing for her audience as when a child is being loved by a circle of grown-ups. And like a child, she was kicking the toe of her left sneaker against the raised heel of her right one, her broad face lit up like fire. Faith sucked in a wet breath with her tongue against her teeth, making a slight sucking noise. Her hair was down, bouncing loose in a long full bloom; nothing held it or her in. For a moment, I stood awestruck.

Then against my will, my face tightened as if its skin were a stretched nylon. Students were holding up signs like "women of the world unite," "sisterhood is power," and "justice for women now." Some of the women were shouting, some were silent, all were young, most in John Lennon caps and dungarees. A beautiful young woman with startling red hair was shouting through a megaphone. "We can do it! Yes, we can! The bus is at

Andrews' entrance gate! We are one!" and the others applauded.

Moving away, I felt myself trip on something. Some young woman had put her books and notebook down on the floor and I stumbled over them. A pain pierced through my ankle as I tumbled; I cried out and then put my hand over my mouth. I felt an abrasion and cut bleed through my ankle skin. Three girls looked down at me without stopping. Then the fourth girl kneeled. "You all right? Can I help you stand?"

I let the girl help me to my feet. I looked down at the skid of strawberry jam on the floor. I had knocked down the jar when I had tried to hold onto the counter for balance. It had fallen with me from a kitchen counter. "Hells Bells!" the girl said. "That must hurt."

"Thank you very much —" I said abashed. "Thank you." Slowly, beyond, the crowd was thickening.

I pushed through the crowd to get to Faith's office as my ankle was throbbing — I did not know how or where I would find the balance.

I popped my head into Faith's office and she waved at me, saying, "Oh, honey, I completely forgot! Come back later can you?" She turned to the girl she had been speaking with instead, the girl's pages strewn out on Faith's desk, not mine. I felt my disappointment, like a sharp light piercing both my eyes, I was burning with pain.

I took the shortest route possible to the center of town; cars whizzed past me toward White Plains or New York City. And, needing relief, I ached now for a warm burst of Macallan's Scotch in my gut. I thought only briefly about the women on the march holding their homemade placards. My ankle had stopped throbbing, but still, I walked with difficulty. By the time I reached the center of the small town, I was ravenous for a drink.

The red-orange brick walkway with oak trees and stone pots on the edge led to the town's specialty stores behind bright green but small awnings. I quickly walked into the small liquor store as if no longer tethered to those moments at Faith Hale's office.

"Twelve-year Macallan," I said to the storeowner, as he picked through a row on which the different scotches rested, the bottles more comfortable with my presence I thought, than the very formal storeowner himself who eventually rang me up with some doubt as to whether to ask me for an ID. He watched me leave with a full bottle of the spicy liquor. A twelve-year Macallan, I read from the label. Twelve meant that almost half my life had been in sync with the scotch's aging process and I was about to drink from a younger brother in a way. I laughed at this thought, suddenly remembering how my father held such bottles of Macallan in such close embrace; they each could have been one of his children. What would my father think about Faith Hale? Would he tell me Faith hadn't meant to forget me again and again? Or maybe he would say Faith Hale was nothing but a famous phony who used politics for personal fame and who gave her adulation and attention to anyone, like she was doing when I had wanted so badly that she talk with me about my writing? My father. . .who removed his suit jacket and meticulously hung it over the black horsehair chair in the living room where the liquor cabinet resided, antique and creaky, with a latch that looked as old as its colonial oakwood. Everything in the living room was as gracefully refined as my father, including the twelve-year Macallan's with a picture of a Scottish mansion on its bottle. Drinking Macallan's Scotch, for my father, had been one of the joys of his life, and as I held the bottle, I found myself walking to the waters under the cement footbridge overhanging the streaming Bronx River. The question tormented me. Had Faith actually forgotten, or maybe Faith couldn't have helped it. . .again? Or, maybe, just maybe, it was me?

The river water was shallow under the locust trees. The ripples made the water look like it was hiccupping; tiny bursts of frothy bubbles sprang up. It was different from the water of my swimming pool in Pound Ridge, which had smelled of chlorine. Where the river got deeper, the gray-brown became darker and I stared into it, watching the hiccups turn more into small brownish-white curls. The river went all the way into the Bronx, someone had once told me. But thinking of the Bronx only made me think again of Faith. Beyond the Bronx lay the bustling recklessness of Manhattan whose freedom and gracious, noisy anonymity I missed. I unscrewed the cork-lined cap of the Macallan's and took in two sips of the scotch, feeling its familiar pungency fall through and within me, and soon, after a few more swigs, I was light-headed. I bent to remove my sneakers and sweatsocks to go sit down under the footbridge where the silt was almost soft as clay, and there were a few gray jutting rocks I could sit on without falling into the sludge.

I looked down at the river and remembered Cape Elizabeth, my father swept into the sea waves, and then I didn't remember what I felt then but numbness, and a lightless world.

I had long started wondering: was suicide justifiable? Why did my father do it? Because he was unhappy with his life, was how I had answered my own question. Because he was weak and in pain. Because he thought he was invisible and nothing. Because the dark states when they fell like they might have been at that moment were an unbeatable purgatory. Because he was so tired of fighting the dark states.

I settled myself on one of the jutting rocks and took more sips of the Macallan, hoping the dark states would not now descend like a prisoner's chains. My thoughts felt scattered and diffused, as if I had just woken up from a sleep in an early morning where nobody and nothing but my isolated thoughts occupied the dawn. As much as I wanted to just forget about Faith Hale, I felt repeatedly pulled into the possibility of cure by Faith and release of these impending dark states, as if her spell had not so much been broken, but just took up more space in the universe.

When my father came to my bedroom to read me passages from Marcel Proust, I had looked at him sometimes with pity. Yet it all confused me too; so handsome and brilliant and different, he offered me an outsiderdom that was both exquisite and strange but could be fatal.

There had been no place for my dark states in the splendor, the exquisiteness of pine and birch and willow trees, rock gardens and stonewalls, delicate flowers with their tangerine and light blue colors in the town of Pound Ridge. Maybe Faith Hale would still care about all this? She had read my work — the dark states in my words had been in it.

It was always my father, whose thinner, paler personality I fell into the arms of, almost like a lover, going to sleep by him knowing of my mother's blatant absence. I had almost stopped believing that my dark states would ever stop after I almost drowned myself in the swimming pool down the driveway. That was one spring evening in 1971, after sitting in the kitchen sipping a ginger ale mixed with whole milk and chocolate syrup. The drink was a treat my father had introduced me to and for which, after much pleading from me, Sofia had reluctantly purchased six-packs of Canada Dry Ginger

Ale to keep on the pantry floor. I had been missing my
father so much that evening. The spring moon seemed
to be warming me, then. As I had many times after my
father drowned, I was imagining death as a dark hope of
meeting him again.

The dark states were threatening to return if I didn't
hold onto Faith's spell, I thought. But Faith still could
make it different for me, I told myself. And hadn't she
already taken an interest in me even though she was so
busy with others? Hadn't she read the parts in the book
about the dark states and their fierceness and not re-
coiled from them as I was sure Dickers had? Taking a sip
of the Macallan, I felt the autumn on my face. If Faith
was back, I could hold onto something I still couldn't
explain to myself. There was nothing I could remember
reading that described this kind of need I had for Faith,
and the unfamiliarity frightened me.

The Proust! Did my father leave the Proust anywhere for me? "'Then, suddenly, my anxiety subsided,'"
my father once read to me from Proust's *Swann's Way*,
a threadbare, stitched volume the color of rye bread, a
1924 edition he kept in his study. "'I had formed a res-
olution to abandon all attempts to go to sleep without
seeing Mamma, and had decided to kiss her at all costs,
even with the certainty of being in disgrace with her
for long afterwards, when she came up to bed. . .and like
a ripe fruit which bursts through its skin, was going to
pour out into my intoxicated heart the gushing sweetness
of Mamma's attention. . .'"

My thoughts continued to soar. And I was remembering bits and snatches of life with my father.

If I didn't hold onto Faith's spell, it would all be
gone. Then, I knew, if I dipped my hand into the water,
it would be cold to the touch, and would smell muddy
and sweet, and then it would no longer be a place of

shame in yearning for Mamma's kiss, but a reminder, a hope of relief. Suddenly Faith had stood there with the presence of the river water, like an apparition. My fears and hopes rested side by side in combat with one another.

I had wondered one night: compared to my seductive mother, I could have been a blur of undifferentiated bone and flesh. Sofia's dancer body entered my dream life as a haunting. In the dreams, it was as if Sofia's large breasts were hammers, and they pounded into the corners of my consciousness, telling me my father and I were worthless.

Another night I had this dream about Sofia, and it was she who was caressing me. The world was turned upside down. And then I thought of my father and the library, and I calmed. I pulled out of the dream, awakening so thirsty my mouth felt like it had been sucking on steel nails, and my body had turned into one muscle expelling my mother from itself. And the thought of her wide-open station of sex, sucking at me all around remained. I wondered but knew Sofia would know exactly how to be with Dickers; he would be attracted to my mother's breasts. And now my mind was traveling backward where in high school memories I saw myself with a friend named Mary Leathers. We were drunk on ripple wine in the woods behind the high school, singing Country Joe and the Fish songs and telling each other the secrets of sex we had recently learned — mine of having one of Sofia's boyfriends feel me up on the living room couch when she was in her dancing studio. Chris Moran, with his beer-soaked words and slur and beauty, was a tall sandy-blond eighteen-year-old who always walked with a six-pack of Schlitz beer under one of his arms, and who had licked my right breast, and whose saliva felt good and warm, even with the beer stink on his breath. I had marked the spot on the couch furtively by putting a price sticker that I tore off the six-pack he had put on the floor, lifting up a cushion where we had laid, I under him, his large hand under my shirt. Remembering Chris Moran and the feeling of getting felt up had made me feel attractive for the first time in my life, like I had been marked with worth. I wanted to tell my mother that I had experienced something sweet and tender. But where was my mother that day? And hadn't I seen her later in the barn with the same boy who had given me such completion, the same Chris Moran? When I went to look through the colonial window of the barn, I saw her, with him, with Chris Moran, her lean legs on the balcony, and they were doing it too. And the air was filled with shocks.

When I was much younger, I had beckoned all sorts of female material into my bed before I got a doll named Marie: wool sweaters, skirts, tights, all to feel some "maternal" warmth against my skin. I did not mind my bed filled with clothes as replacements for the warm flesh of my mother and waited until early morning to replace them in the bedroom drawers before Sofia rose to beckon breakfast. I learned that the tights and the dark woolen skirts my mother bought me when I shopped in the town's exclusive boutiques brought the most comfort in my bed.

I was ten in 1962 and a guest was over for dinner. I would remember always the discussion that night. It was about Lyndon Johnson, and our guest was the famous and popular novelist, Rod Barker, with bristly short black hair, who wore leopard-skinned bedroom slippers even out for dinner and was to have his popular *Eleventh Precinct* detective series bound in expensive Florentine leather with a gold binding. He spoke over my father at a dinner, but Sofia was so taken in by the guest who was handsome even though his skin was pockmarked from childhood acne. He still had his Bronx accent from his Italian family who came from Sicily. I had heard their voices and teasing from behind the bathroom door later, Sofia's and Mr. Barker's — who had his name changed to Barker from the Italian name DeLillo. They had stolen away from the dining table into the hall bathroom at eight thirty, before dessert, leaving my father and me there. I went to see where they might have gone then saw through the crack — the door left only partially closed — my mother's bra straps were around her elbows. My mother had on a high-waisted yellow dress that evening and the yellow looked orange in the bathroom light mixing in with the moon from the window. Sofia had slipped off her high heels for him so she wouldn't be taller and his hand was on one of the loose cups of Sofia's bra. "Shit," Mr. Barker said, when he saw me. His penis wasn't out but now I saw he had pulled down Sofia's brassiere and her bosoms bounced like two tennis balls.

The three of them sat at the dining table for dessert, with me silent after the encounter, as if nothing had happened. Edward's eyes moistened, as if he had known, his face grave and stricken. But not a word was spoken among the four of us. The maid, Adeline, opened the dining room window, as if she knew, too, and was trying to let the wind wash it all away.

I thought I understood my father's darkness after that. Though nothing was ever said of the incident with Rod Barker.

As I sat at the river, remembering all this in short spurts of scenes, I looked down at the thigh I had once cut. There were scars under my blue jeans from my cutting. Since the emergency room at Cape Elizabeth, I had not cut myself again, and the scars were ridged and brown, which I thumbed when I was anxious. The color had slowly turned to pale from pink, and the scars had flattened, but they were still bumpy.

I would see Faith again and alone, I reassured myself. Faith would apologize for forgetting me, sometime, I told myself. She wasn't like my mother, not in body or self. And there could be some order and meaning and cure to these dark memories and thoughts. Faith still had the spell, didn't she? I let out a long breath of relief. There had to be hope. I couldn't give up that easily. That rainy night in Faith's office was as real as the rocks around me, wasn't it? And wasn't Faith "loving" my novel about my life? She couldn't be a liar. She wouldn't be Faith Hale if she was.

It was Barbara Rubin, my roommate from the Neighborhood Playhouse, who took me to the East River to watch the ducks jump up and dive back in, their thin necks tucked and held tight to their chests. "The baby ducks," Barbara said, "imprint onto the big mother ones, and follow them like lost children waddling through the shore." And now, of the ducks, I thought: What if I had helplessly and unknowingly imprinted onto Faith Hale? What if that was what the spell was? What if there was another answer to the neat psychologies that I had heard in the psychiatrists' offices in Westport where Sofia sent me after I cut myself? What if I could actually attain Proust's "Mamma's kiss?" Would that be a cure for the dark states instead of the stuffy old psychiatrists my mother hired to treat me in therapy sessions heavy with boredom? And it was that simple. What if some form of Proust's "Mamma's kiss" could, at last, halt the dark states and chase them far away? Forever.

I looked into the river waters. A Pandora's box filled with images colliding with each other under opposite

emotional pulls fell on me, images of Faith's sturdy arms
and face that first night in the rain when I had come to
her office. I remembered the hope; how could I give up
the hope? Then I thought of the aroused crowd around
Faith's office today, excluding me. Did it really matter
that Faith was like this, there always being dens of other women desiring her attentions, too? She was Faith
Hale after all. I told myself that. And I could learn the
politics. I could have my own political sign and place; it
didn't matter how many she had held.

My mind went back Barbara Rubin. What would
the thick crowd of protestors think about poor Barbara Rubin? About the "sisterhood" she and I had. How
did Barbara fit into the general national "sisterhood"
with women now in their elegant blue-jeaned make-
up-lessness?

Barbara Rubin and the omelets. . .. Barbara's hands
were so small, I could slip Barbara's fingers under my
own and keep them in a tight fold, as if protecting Barbara from more men, and the pungent sex smell she always
had on her clothes. How innocent our holding of each
other was, like two sisters in a stormy household with
an evil father and mother. We two found some peace
and companionship, and that was all. Except I copied
Barbara's copious makeup style, laying great streaks of
pancake makeup on my face and painting my eyelids
with blue eyeliner and a black eyebrow pencil. It brought
me closer to Barbara, and I still felt a certain companionship in these cheapening effects which were defining
me. I washed my makeup off once I knew I was going
to Abigail Stone and now went like the other female
students naked of makeup, in jeans and a pullover, and
sneakers.

Looking down at the flowing river, I thought school
was a boat and I was only a passenger on it. At any time,

I could be deported and have to go back home to Sofia. I also wondered how far could a person swim out toward New York City before they were finally taken by the deeper waves?

Chapter Five.

I picked up my pace, staring into the yellow and white dorm houses on the way back to my own dorm, Garrison, before I decided I wouldn't go back yet to my room. Not yet, I thought.

It was late afternoon, and the clouds looked thirsty and thin. If I went back to my dorm room, I would have to think of Dickers again, the compromised afternoon and the feelings not of nausea or regret but of mortification. I would have to work up my hope again, and what if it would instead dissolve just by remembering what had happened in Dickers's office? Then I realized I would have to go to his office again at least three more times before Faith was to come back. I did not know if I could fake such adoration again, work up such a game of eroticized admiration. It wasn't that I felt only erased by such a display of fawning on my part; it's that I suddenly felt servile and dirty. That his soul was more like a canister of one of my mother's old Electrolox vacuum cleaners, full of dusty and hot air. That there was a kind of a cruelty in the otherwise mild-mannered, fatherly gentleman whom I could also feel sorry for. Except for when he enjoyed the delight of affairs with younger women, he seemed to enjoy the time and space he spent on his own thoughts, that forest of self-centered abstractions. He might find himself lost in an isolation like I was, I thought, after he hung up the phone on his agent and he was alone again. But what of me now?

The college library was small, packed into a dormitory building, with its stacks of books in tilting sequences along old cedar wood shelves. If I couldn't be with Faith for now, I would console myself in the solitary comfort of this small Abigail Stone College library and its texts. The library — all those books and texts and all that silence. I read the latest Abigail Stone College newspaper, telling me there wasn't enough room in the law schools for the large number of female students applying to change the world. Then I read that there had been a symposium on the "nuclear family" and how little these new students were engaged in it, being now miles away from the limitations their parents experienced in their day. And what should the college do about this? About the changing needs for women who need other women while in college and for life?

I hadn't seen Faith Hale since that awful day when Faith had forgotten me for a second time in her office.

Each time I went to the library to bury myself in books the long days after the incident with Dickers and the wait to see Faith again, I bought myself a toasted tunafish sandwich from the campus pub, and a tangy, soothing odor permeated the air around me as I rifled through pages and pages of texts for my psychology classes. I hardly thought of Dickers there, but I did think of Faith and how we would be together even after all that happened. It felt good to skip the crowded Bates dining room. The librarian didn't ask me to remove the sandwich or throw it away, and slowly I could feel the food filling my stomach with a satiety I didn't feel elsewhere. This librarian, a mother from the town of

Bronxville, always sat at a desk in the back. Her fingernails were painted a deep maroon, which reminded me of Mrs. Leathers back in Bedford, whose nail polish always shone through the darkness whenever she came in the bedroom to say good night and shut off the light when I was having a sleepover with Mary, her tongue sticking out slightly between her teeth as she smiled.

A combination of motherly guard and protector, I always showed the librarian my student ID, at which the woman gave a grand gesture with her hand, indicating that the room was mine and I wouldn't be bothered.

I found a place behind a long cedar desk, where I lay my sandwich down to begin my research. Soon, I connected the mayonnaise odor from my sandwiches with the library's old wood smells, the librarian's smile and gesturing, and the smells of textbooks and nonfiction books, and then with a sense of genuine, lasting hope. I spent time at the library, gathering texts in a room like my father's warm carpeted library, the "magic kingdom" as I called it as a child. After finishing my sandwich, I would go downstairs to the ladies room and wet a towel and then swipe out another, that one fresh and dry. Then, up in the library again, I used the wet cloth to clean up any crumbs or bits the sandwich may have left, drying it with the other towel. My corner was to be kept clean, I told myself, so as not to anger the librarian.

I loved the firm feel of the texts; I loved the concrete certain thingness of them. They were solid and strong. And my anxious states became subdued for a while. Texts were like solitude itself, I thought, like being alone without regret, and without fear. It was the one thing Dickers had been right about. Then, thinking of Dickers, my body suddenly felt like the world was a place of unknowable sorrow.

After a few days in the library, I read a short biography of Faith Hale in a Jewish journal where I looked through archives to learn more about the woman who had put such a spell on me.

Faith Hale's parents were Moldavian socialists, I learned. Her paternal uncle had been murdered by the Czarist Police. Her parents had been arrested for joining workers' demonstrations and shouting out protests against Czarist Russia. Faith's mother had been exiled to Siberia and her father was jailed in Russia. They were released after the revolution and immigrated to New York City, where Faith was born in the 1920s. In 1942, Faith married Richard Hale. They had two children — Grace, born in 1949, and Isaac, born in 1951. The couple divorced in 1962, the same year in which she married Ralph Peters, a family friend and political ally. A short story writer of many honors, Hale is known widely, too, as a political activist, a role that began, as it might have for many of the characters she has created in her short stories, as a result of PTA activities in her daughter's school, one article said. She had been in jail, arrested for a peace protest on New York City's West Side. The combination of personal and large world concerns created for her a prominent role in the peace movement of the 1960s, about which she wrote her famous essay, "That Man from the USA Flying over Hanoi is a Murderer."

I had to interrupt my reading to attend classes. In one class, "The Psychology of Creativity," I sat in a claustrophobic room, quiet and listening, as a girl with bulbous eyes wearing a motorcycle jacket argued against the robotic insult of Skinner's sparse behavioral psychology. Then there was "Modern Literature" where they read a book called *The Dwarf,* in which I relished the lines like, "I have noticed that sometimes I frighten people; what they really fear is themselves. They think it is I who scare them, but it is the dwarf within them, the ape-faced manlike being who sticks up his head from the depths of their souls."

I felt oddly whole, quietly myself in these classes but finding myself also comforted by the abstract ideas and sometimes heated discussions I listened to hungrily. The small intimate classes where I sat and absorbed texts and ideas like a shadow who had made sure the light was not on me, but whose own substance lay behind a brainy shyness strong as the bright student's verbiage. When I saw Faith again, I would tell her of my absorption in this world, and all would be possible again. But all the while, I yearned to return to my reading in the library.

Then, back in the library one day, I found a long section on the phenomenon called "imprinting" in one of my psychology books, *Introduction to Psychology.*

I wrote it down in my notebook. It was like finding a door to a mountain, the inexplicable explained. Case studies showed that the "imprinting" figure "looms as you awaken after you have experienced a kind of death, a hopelessness, from a destructive maternal figure. And that the "imprint" substitute mother figure is the first step toward what the book said was "the hazardous process of reintegration of self." Whatever that meant, I thought. I didn't know, but it sounded better than my unease and the emptiness I felt within myself before I met Faith Hale. And maybe the dark states could be relinquished by this stronger, elusive entity. If I "imprinted" on Faith, could it be that the void where an emotional and mental virus haunted and tormented me could be defeated? That darkness and suicide was not my destiny as it had been for my father?

"Faith," I wrote in my notebook. . .a kind of salvation, the mysterious, mystical, and magical workings of the unconscious." Now there was a plan forming in my head. I asked myself again: Was there a cure for me and the dark states by imprinting onto this presence, Faith Hale, even more fully? Could the dark states at least be stopped repeatedly by imprinting on Faith? How long would it take for the imprint to be branded into me? It was an absurd idea, I told myself, but no less precious to me as a plan. That I could be someone else, not this Allegra. That's what an imprint could rescue me from. And that such a planting of effects had happened on one rainy night, in a room with this unusual, powerful woman named Faith Hale. I felt something had been explained by these definitions — an explanation of what happened to me that night I met Faith. I couldn't help myself. If I imprinted onto Faith Hale, there was hope against the black sun, despair, and the looming pull of suicide. Against the pull to join my father. Could the dark states be finally banished? It was the first hope I had had in such a long time.

In the library, I also read more history that I could use in my novel. I read from the microfilm about Jane Alpert, as much a woman warrior my same age, as I was a shy, uncomfortable, messy girl. On Novemeber 12, 1969, a bomb had exploded in the Criminal Courts building, a microfilm of the *New York Times* newspaper article reported. It had happened at around 2 am, and the young woman, Jane Alpert, telephoned police headquarters after she planted it, to warn them to evacuate the building.

While trying to absorb details of the story, as if against my own will, I had found myself instead drawn to an advertisement on the opposite page. It glared up at me, like fiery eyes: "At Lord and Taylor, the beautiful people's boots have arrived!" The ad announced. "The finest feathers, the softest suede. Really more like leather stockings than boots which, aided by higher heels, makes legs look miraculously lithe and lean!" The girl, Jane Alpert, in the babushka, taken in handcuffs to the

Women's House of Detention under the headline "Court Building Bombed; F.B.I. Seizes 2 at Armory" seemed remote and unreal.

After a few days in the library, I began to read the "feminist" books, the newest ones, and the *Ms.* magazines scattered on tables. The first preview issue of *Ms.* magazine, a "new magazine for women" captured my attention one afternoon. About to take a break from researching Jane Alpert, I noticed its red cover with a cone-shaped figure of a woman bearing eight bright blue arms streaming out of her torso. A female octopus. I remembered the octopus in Dickers's novel, the tentacles ripping off a bathing suit on an innocent woman's body so that the woman was naked and swimming helplessly in a pool alone. The *Ms.* magazine cover was like an alternate mythical being, who in each hand instead held an object of considerable weight and was herself the octopus. Her face was stained with huge tears flowing in white dots. The woman was holding, successively, a watch, a feather duster, a skillet with an egg frying on it, a manual typewriter, an iron, a car's steering wheel, a hand mirror, a telephone, a graphic of a naked baby pictured inside an egg bubble under her waist, and a picture of a cat by her left leg. The woman struggled as she tried to keep her balance under the weight of these objects while wearing high heels. I looked to the woman at the front desk, at the back of her housewifey coiffed hair, and felt a strange but sympathetic itch to know more about her, to know more about myself, too, as if the spread of *Ms.* magazines and their sundry covers had an orphic pull of sorts, if not of my own image, but of the images of the women I had known in Westchester; housewives holding what looked like hundreds of chores and duties like the octopus woman on the cover, and mothers of my friends, with whom I was at least partly connected by my sex, but I didn't know — or didn't know yet — what to make of those connections. I seemed at that time, instead, floating in my own stillness, the frightening open-endedness of my own future and fate. I thought of the power Faith had for me, of being embraced by that power, of the inevitability of meeting with Faith again and correcting what had happened in my yearnings. It would be all right again if only I could believe that Faith would be there. I was, with this octopus, Faith Hale, not naked and stranded in a pool helpless and humiliated. The excitement of finding part of myself in the new images began to heal the infringement Dickers's rejection of my breasts made onto my body, those breasts, hungry for touch. How did I fit into all this feminist stuff? I didn't know, but only that I did, and I found a startling cessation of anxiety holding the magazines in my own hands and reading them. I would write this quote from Robin Morgan in my journal: "Participatory democracy begins at home. If you are planning to implement your politics, there are certain things to remember."

"You change by participation, constant self-analysis, struggle with yourself. . .confess your backwardness, your inadequacies. Eventually your whole personality can change your way of looking at the world."

In the first few pages of *Ms.* magazine, I read the letters:

> Upon reading the article "Body Hair, the Last Frontier," I was reminded of an incident. In 1967 while I was teaching civilian volunteers on their way to work in Southeast Asia, I was approached by a colleague with a serious request. Would I, he asked, spare one of his classes of military types some embarrassment by

telling 'that girl' in one of my classes of types that she must shave the long, black hair on her legs before going abroad: its presence would be damaging to the image of the United States. No feminist then, my reaction was still immediate outrage. No, I would not say anything to her. The hair on anyone's legs is strictly their own business.
Rebecca L. Moreton

Among the articles that I really enjoyed was Germaine Greer's "Down With Panties!" As a matter of fact, the next day I decided to stop wearing shorts. They're hot and they creep up on me while I'm walking and when I'm just standing, they inhibit my natural appearance. That night I went to a party — sans shorts. I felt like Tarzan — the naked truth.
Jack D. White

Hurrah! At last, a magazine I can read without cringing. *Ms.* is a joy! About Germaine Greer's article against panties whether I wear panties, is about as important to me as whether I burned my bra. Which is not at all. Neither my breasts nor my bottom direct my mind, and my "consciousness" will not be raised higher by freeing those parts of my anatomy.
Marcia Cord

This new world I was finding myself in was dizzying. I tried to bury myself in my new novel trying
to write in the first person, as someone with high
moral purposes, taking on Jane Alpert's warrior self
and imagining myself with Alpert's babushka and as
a lean and shadowy figure. She was a girl on the edge
of time, Jane Alpert, I thought. Then I suddenly
realized, that was myself, Allegra, too. "Feminism,"
I scribbled in my notebook, ". . .it's like you're jumping from a ledge and there's a net to catch you, it's
made from the entangled threads of other women's
pasts, hopes, futures, and fates."

Amid the *Ms.* magazines, and the bold paperback
copies of *Sisterhood Is Powerful* (like I saw in the abortion
doctor's room), I was teetering at the tip of a strange,
changing new world. The microfilm brought the images
of Jane Alpert and the other two male bombers flashing
up to me through the viewer. They shocked me like the
ubiquitous anti-war posters on the onion-colored walls
in the library, in the pub, and up on dormitory walls
throughout the college.

But who was I amid all these signs and symbols?
What girl against the background of both violence and
identity?

In the last few pages of *Ms.* magazine. I read this:

American Women's Petition

Support the American Women's Petition
and its signers below in a campaign to
change the attitude and laws against
abortion in this country.

And there was Faith Hale's signature among the
other famous signers.

I saw the pamphlets from "The War Resister's League" in the library too. It was an organization Faith was famous for being part of. And in my reading about the early revolutionary, radical seventies bombers and the dirty floors of a railroad apartment in the East Village where the dynamite for the bombs had been kept in the refrigerator (according to newspaper reports), I envisioned instead the other reflection of the "movement," in Faith's West Village near Washington Square. From different stories about Faith that I read from biographical synopses tagged onto the pamphlets and announcements on the library display tables, I learned that the "movement" sprung from PTA meetings and community centers holding anti-war and consciousness-raising meetings full of housewives — the obverse reflection of their violent counterpart in downtown revolutionary groups like Jane Alpert's. The Abigail Stone College student magazine published some of Faith Hale's older essays from Hanoi, after she was chosen to go there by the War Resister's League. Photographs and fliers were tacked up on the library's bulletin board, just as Faith's public readings had been.

I couldn't stand to see them, the harsh war protest language and the woman I yearned for in a large circle of fellow anti-war protestors. Faith's large face solemn, her brown eyes intensely open as if witnessing executions. I had not yet seen Faith's face as serious as when I looked at those posters which boldly spelled out: "Attend a talk on prisoners of war in Vietnam, Faith Hale, December 6." But, as with everything, I didn't understand and was just beginning to learn about the shadowed, far away life where I had heard Faith gathered with her many friends at the Peace Center in basements and lofts, storefronts, and churches. I stooped to read one of Faith's quotes, as there were pamphlets on the library table and short clippings under the announcements of organized antiwar marches.

One afternoon, I picked up one of the pamphlets, to take something of Faith's for what was going to be, I knew, a longer wait, if I had the courage to confront Faith at all. I read from the pamphlet the text:

"Thieu Thi Tao could have been one of my daughters. Thieu was beaten on the head with truncheons, her head was between with two steel bars. It was my American government that did this. . ."

The world seemed larger with Faith Hale in it, and safer and protected from perpetrators, men, and the violence. As if it could house even my psychological hungers.

I could not stop thinking of Faith. Or about how Faith acted when I had tried to keep the meeting in her office. What was my plan now?

Searching for a new pen in the college bookstore a week later, Faith still wasn't back, but I came upon Faith's book of short stories with a shock. Its sober light brown cover with its title in capital red letters belied the unstuffy personality of its writer, and I took it from the shelf gingerly. On the back of the cover were quotes from writers like Philip Roth and Joseph Heller, and it frightened me how important the book felt. I held Faith's book with the same oppressing feelings of admiration and smallness I felt when admiring Sofia. But when, on the back — with the quotes, I saw the author's photo, the wide, warm face — instead of putting it down, a hope was lit again inside me. I found myself grabbing a pen off the shelf near it, and I took Faith's book to the cashier to buy.

Later that night, I read from Faith's collection
of short stories — I took the book into bed with
me — and a force nailed me, either in admiration or
dismay, and the force would not let me go. I needed
to find Faith. I was restless with a new urgency.
Opening my underwear drawer, I removed the notebook Faith had given me and I wrote my first entry
of what would be many long entries the next day and
the days to come.

I wrote about meeting Faith Hale, the Neighborhood Playhouse, and Barbara. And I started to date
each entry.

October 8.

There is a realm where my father lives,
tender, with his books and stricken face:
reality always bothered him. I imagine
he, my father, still a presence in my
life, calling me to walk among stones
and water and telling me he will catch
me before I fall. I feel him in my night
swims through memory.

I fixed up my room for the notebooks, cleaning
spaces next to the bureau and weak-legged desk to make
room for them. I bought Borax in town and sprinkled it
all around the room to entrap the ants. I would tell Faith
about the journal when we met up again.

One morning, two weeks after seeing the crowd of students in Faith's office and seeing Faith for that one painful glimpse, I awoke to the smell of a sulfurous smoke.

I panicked and threw the sheet off me, thinking it was my own body burning, but there was smoke crawling through the crack under the door. I hurried to the window, yanking the curtain to expose the wet morning. It must have been only eight o'clock, I thought. A few students had spilled out of their rooms into the morning, scared too by the smoke and burnt fibers — which I realized must have been coming from the back lounge. I recognized the lounge's old mattress, laid out in the rain, black from smoke. The tiny fire was out; buckets of water and the rain had been enough to douse it. Two lesbian students were out, kissing each other, sharing a blanket over their shoulders and laughing. I watched these two women under the sun's cloudy light, and I watched as three college guards pulled the smoking mattress further out in the rain, toward the big rock on the campus walkway. Then, in the distance, I saw Faith. Faith was passing out tangerines, hugging and consoling the scattered crowd. It was clear that I wasn't imagining Faith. I pulled my jeans on and buckled them at my waist. I pulled on a mohair sweater without putting a shirt underneath. Sockless and shoeless, I pulled open the door, where the odors of lovemaking from the back lounge, where the mattress had caught fire, seemed to assail me with cheap wine and cigarettes. Suddenly, I remembered the dream I had the night before. I had dreamed of lying on top of the river, as if the water were hard glass and I could safely fall asleep there under the moon and not be drowned.

Outside now, the morning was cool — I wasn't cold even barefoot. There Faith was on this rainy morning, passing out her tangerines. She stood a few yards away on the stone wall closer to the administration building. She was talking to the two young women who had been kissing, and I watched her as she rifled through the thick, unruly hair of one of the lesbians. Why was Faith there? They were sitting so close, Faith and the girl. Faith turned suddenly, as if all that stood now as she watched the girl Faith had been talking to go back to her friend, was coming to a finish. Then in a few minutes I felt myself walking to Faith. The other women had left and Faith was alone. The long wait was over, I thought, even before she spoke. It happened like that; in seconds and in smoke, my life was about to be changed.

"Why did you leave? It would have been good for you to stay. I wanted to talk to you about your pages, Allegra." Faith suddenly said to me. I could hardly believe she was there, talking to me. It was more that I let myself believe it. Faith jumped off the stone wall, hitting the ground with a soft thump, which made me laugh. "I used to be thinner around some places," she joked. "Now when I land, I can feel the Earth asking, what weight is this suddenly upon me?" I pushed out a forced laugh, but then I was crying.

"I have things to say to you," Faith said, more serious than I had expected or ever heard her speak. "I don't know why you left that day."

"I didn't know anybody there," I said clumsily, hoping Faith would not notice my tears.

"Yeah? Well, you knew me. Walk with me now. I want to talk to you about your story. I know you won't leave so abruptly, right?"

"Right," I said, and I let myself follow Faith up to Andrews, up through the path that went to the big white door, and we were in the hallway with the staircase and chandelier again and a sudden sharp slap of memory hit my face so that I was reddening.

"I know. I understand," Faith said. "Come on." She was motioning me to follow her once again through the empty classroom, the dusty kitchen, and when Faith opened the door to her office, I let out a breath that was relieved and anxious all at the same time.

"See, I have it," Faith said, motioning me to sit where there were pillows on the window sill. "Talk to me, darling." I saw my pages on her desk, as Faith pulled them out from a pile of others and put one page in front of her eyes. She wasn't reading it for the first time, I noticed, and it was serious, the mood, the tenor of Faith's voice, her brown eyes enlarging as if they were becoming two bulbs of light. "So this is the darkness inside you. . ." Faith said slowly, and I looked speechlessly at her.

"My mother died when I was just a kid," Faith said. "You know what I did when I heard she had cancer? I hid in her dress closet so she wouldn't know I was in the room when the doctor told her. I was very sad and depressed a good while after she died."

"No, my father. . ."

"I know what he did. You wrote about it beautifully. It is beautiful what you've written here. Yeah, Maine, I used to go up there, a while ago. Don, my husband, and I now go to eastern Vermont, only because Don has a farmhouse there. I should go there now — just to think, you know. Think things through, as they say. And the abortion, I can't tell you how important it is that these stories now be told."

Suddenly, I felt as if something serious had happened that Faith wasn't telling me. Faith's face had turned pale when talking about her mother and her cancer. What did Faith have to "think through?"

I watched Faith stare at me, bewildered that I wasn't talking back to her. "No, no," Faith said. "I meant when I married my husband, Don, since he has a family farmhouse in Thetford, when I leave the city it's to be in Vermont, not Maine. No, not any longer. I don't have anything against Maine, if that's what you're thinking —"

"No, Mrs. Hale — I mean, Faith. I understand."

"So your pages here, how much of the story do you think you have?"

"I honestly don't know," I said very softly.

"Whatever it is. A little or enormous, look it over again, darling, and you will see for yourself it means something. In the writing sphere, I mean. The writing is good."

"I. . ."

"It wasn't a question. The writing is first-class writing. I was reading it and I said, this is first class."

"Thank you, Mrs. — Faith."

"Yeah, call me Faith by now." There was now a tough Bronx accent that came with her talking, as if she decided just at that moment to give the visibly scared me some emotional room to stop fearing her.

"Listen to me; don't listen to other people."

"OK," I said tentatively, then Faith all at once came right up to me and pulled me against her breasty chest, and she smelled like tangerines and the morning rain, and I felt a sudden, serious fatigue which, if I could sleep, would feel good. If I could sleep after this long, long time of waiting just for these moments with Faith. . ..

"OK, Cookie." Faith said when she finally let me go. "You can come into my class next semester. Or this semester, if you like."

My head felt strangely light, and I breathed deeply.

"Look, I'm reading at six. Come and we can even talk more, Toots — afterward. I have to do a couple of things before the reading. Take your pages. Oh, by the way, do you know anything about blush?"

"What?"

Faith pulled a small plastic container of deep pink blush out of her desk. "A kid gave me this. No kidding. She was very troubled."

And before I knew it, I was helping Faith look into a round hand mirror and apply the pinkish blush on her cheeks.

"Once, they mistook me for the cleaning lady," Faith told me. "I don't want to look crappy. Is this enough?" She turned her left cheek toward me where she had doused it, and I nodded slowly. And after some red lipstick, Faith was parading around.

"OK, Cookie. Leave me now and go get some nap or sleep or something like that. I'll be in the auditorium around six."

When I reached Garrison, I put my novel pages in my desk drawer for later. I did not undress to lay down but all but flopped down, feeling the exhaustion of the whole anxious week. And I slept soundly, quietly, for what felt like the first time since coming to Abigail Stone College. If not for the dream, everything would have been well. But in the dream, Faith was rolling me on her lap, laughing at me as I looked up in an impulse of terror, dissolving like a stick of butter on a hot pan over her knees. I was terrified. Her eyes were brown and yellow and she could see inside me. And I was helpless. I was being turned into liquid. I woke up and tried reconstructing Faith's face, so that I could see it the way it was in her office that morning. But I struggled to build her image in my mind's eye and to feel her great wreath of warmth around my neck, my shoulders. But then I could hear her lips telling me she loved me, and she loved the words that were freed from inside me now, and no one will ever have the right to object to them. Life is a battle between humiliation and affirmation, she was telling me.

I shook off the dream. It was only a dream, I told myself. I did see and hear Faith earlier that day. That was the reality. I wanted Faith. I needed — Faith. The blackest heart of my despair would be pressed into jewels soon. I would write about those feelings in the dream too, and they weren't sick or perverse, those pulls and feelings, but from some deep void inside me about to be filled. The void where the virus, the suicidal illness, the "depression" all lay and still waited if I didn't accept Faith's love, to take what I had of my life.

I started to get ready — I had time to make it to Faith's reading at six, so I hurried, dressing quickly.

I saw the poster for Faith's appearance tacked onto the auditorium's bulletin board. Faith's image had unfurled inside my mind like a red emergency flag when I got to Reisinger Hall. I followed a line of students into the packed auditorium and found a seat far in the back. Then Faith appeared on the stage like a hallucination.

I had seated myself so far in the back I could hardly make Faith out, but then Faith's voice came through the microphone as she grasped its neck. "Well, I might as well talk into this thing. Wait a minute," Faith was saying. She lifted the microphone up on the pole and the microphone quickly slid down the pole below her waist. She caught it, finally whisked it out of its holder, and said: "I'm not that short, come on."

The audience in the room began to laugh, but it was more like a cheer such as a crowd gives a star athlete whose victories inspired devotion because he was sharing the victories with them.

On the podium, Faith opened a book and smoothed out its pages with the heels of her hands, resting it on the desk-like top of a steel platform that had been placed there for her. The crackle of chewing gum came across the mic and Faith said: "You'll have to excuse me chewing gum, but people who have heard me read before know that I always do. I once lost my voice in the middle of a reading in Albany and ever since then, I do it. After, you can ask questions or make statements in which you give answers and I'll make up the questions, if you want."

There was, again, intense laughter from the audience. I quickly looked around to see if anyone was staring at me, because I had started to cry. Not loud heaves, but tears came, silent and solemn. Embarrassed, I looked down into my lap.

What overwhelmed me in that instant about Faith was the audience's admiration for the gestures which, with both their grace and carelessness, seemed to dismiss playfully a whole culture of formal male readings, by a single, splendid brush of the arm and wash-over of flippant words.

"I'm going to read two pieces," I heard Faith say now. Then I looked up as Faith began her story. Her Queens Bronx enunciations were eloquent on her tongue. Faith did not make contact with the audience with her eyes but with the full thrust of her voice and body. Ringed by darkness because the auditorium lights had been turned off, I could recognize Faith in the main character of the story, in the plain, warm words. The main character, named Grace, spoke with the acrobatic playfulness of Faith's own narrative sentences. Faith read, her performance voice the same as her speaking voice, light-hearted as it floated above the despair of my world, with its sometimes hilarious disobediences before the college's official "writing and literature" students. Faith's elbows balanced her arms as comfortably as possible on the platform, leaning down into the story.

Faith's second selection was a love story. Then I filed out, following the bustling crowd that dispersed, some going to the exit door, and others clamoring to get a word or a look at Faith Hale. I did not stay put. I went to where Faith was surrounded by a hungrily admiring tribe of students. Inching myself slowly toward the crowd around Faith, my face felt tight. But a cluster pulled Faith away from my view quickly. I lost Faith in the tumult.

I stole into my dorm room and picked up the half bottle of scotch I had left over from my last visit to the river. I drank it so fast it burned my throat. I went to the closet, entering it as if I was about to hide there forever. I pulled out the Argentinean blanket Sofia had given me, and it fell across my shoulders. I stayed in the closet for about fifteen minutes until warmed by my thoughts. Would my father be happy I was "intimate" with Faith Hale? I wondered. What would he think?

I left the closet and lay on the bed, my head and its crowding thoughts on the flat pillow. I pushed away a fleeting memory of my afternoon dream. But suddenly, I realized that I had to get to Dickers somehow, to tell him I was leaving him and his class for good. Seeing Faith had, at least, done that.

Chapter Six.

I waited a whole hour, running through my mind what I would tell Dickers. I waited — scared, then finally resolute.

I left my dorm room. I scrambled past the Westlands admission office and up the small hill toward Andrews in the damp after-rain which swelled the evening air.

Then, after going through the classroom adjacent to the kitchen, which was adjacent to Faith's office, I nervously reached Dickers's office, seeing his lamplight on.

I knocked.

"Allegra, right?" he said. He was dressed in pants of durable corduroy and blue as the sky, desert boots, and a lumpy cashmere sweater over his belly.

"I wanted to tell you, Mr. Dickers —" I started. There was a bottle of cheap wine opened on his desk, and he raised his eyebrow after glancing back at it and then to me. His voice was soft as pillows, and it was clear he had had a few drinks, alone.

"Yes, Allegra," he said, quietly but it was in a tone that was flirtatious, as his gaze on me deepened. And now, the way Dickers eyes were looking at me, I realized I would have to talk very fast.

"Are you in town?" He suddenly asked me and then arched his eyebrows again. "Would you like a cup of this red wine? It's not the best," he said.

"No, thank you. I'd like to talk about going to work with Faith Hale." I felt very courageous at that moment, and my voice did not falter, though it changed into a lower tremble.

"Leaving my class, but why?" he asked and, seeing I was not going to come to his desk, he looked like he was reading into my stiffness and silence as an implication that I, too, wanted something of the body to transpire.

He stood opposite me, and his fingers reached for my mother's necklace as it had when I saw him last.

I was going to tell him adamantly again that I was going back to the novel he dismissed. I trembled with all the things I was going to tell him. But, suddenly Dickers simply said, "Will you do me a favor, Allegra?"

"OK," I said, still not moving toward him.

"Please take off your jeans and lie on your back."

And all I could get out was, "Why?"

"Because I want you to. Lie on your back on the carpet, its softer, better." He was the same height as my father had been, though bulkier, and then, in a few seconds I realized, they had the same distinctive Jewish faces. A cruel trick of effects. I could have been dreaming now, a soft veil of dreamy waves rippled over me. He led me, slowly to kneel to the floor and he followed then he bent on both knees, his penis suddenly appearing from behind his zipper like a mole crawling out of a cavern. Did I feel my sex burn a little in want and desire? I didn't know what I felt as I slid off my jeans; I was terrified that he was going to grab the back of my head and push my mouth to his penis, but he slowly unbent my arms, knocked the balance out of me and caught me as I slipped from him, to the floor on my back, and then Dickers, all two hundred and twenty-six pounds, arched over me. The smell of his candy breath, his boredom, drew me out of the illusion that he was gentle and like my own father. I felt my sex panic; then it was as if the rest of my body were swallowing my sex up. I could not feel aroused, only panicked.

Fucking was "a philosophical act of considerable importance," I suddenly remembered he had written about Saul and his androidal wife in his novel, and it would only be for a moment, the discomfort and penetration. I could withstand those things, I told myself — and wouldn't he then call the registrar and get me into Faith's class? Wouldn't this all be the way to Faith?

"I can't stand my own mind," Dickers suddenly said. Then Dickers was actually fucking me; his penis had gone into me. He hadn't yet smelled or noticed the urine starting to flow. His penis went in painlessly, and then my orgasm was a body burp, had I broke wind? I came, looking into the unabashed but bored face of M.B. Dickers. But I was wet all over and not with lovemaking. A rain of urine had fallen down from inside my belly to both my legs, mixing with his semen. Dickers startled off me then. I thought in my mind that my urine had puddled into the office's polished mahogany floorboards, skirted the antique rug, leaving only its outer rim wet, and that, maybe it had landed on his shoes, which he had carefully placed on the sidelines when he first bent towards me to suck his penis. But they were all dry, shielded in their distance between me and Dickers's body and from my urine. Piss and orgasm like some out-of-control animal, and my body tightened in alarm. I still didn't know exactly what had happened, but I had to run. I found my jeans on the floor and pulled them on, and then I ran from the scene — wet and limping and crying out, hearing Dickers muttering "God," through his teeth.

Back in my dorm room, I searched for the spare scotch to murder my shame, my accident. I could feel so drunk soon, I told myself, taking the new bottle of McCallan's out of the closet. The whiskey washed through me again. But I couldn't remember exactly what Dickers had done except for watching me after I wet — he had gotten up for more wine; his face had looked disgusted, hadn't it? Staring into me as I struggled to pull up my jeans, struggled to run as far away as I could from the scene. Rushed out of his office, urine-soaked, semen-dappled, and degraded.

My wetness seemed more acute, as if I had rolled around in a snow bank made of piss, and the world was suddenly devoid of any comfort — the bed in my dorm, the floor of my dorm room where I might place some pillows and the one blanket rolled up on the bedspread until I came back into consciousness and reason.

I went straight to the public showers. I found the shower stall closest to the window, undressed, and turned on the hot water even as it burned — it was better than the burning from my genitals. I leaned into my hand against the bathroom shower wall, turned down the temperature, and let the shower water cascade down my back, my legs. I stood under the pounding water feeling the urine smells dilute until I smelled slightly like a pitcher of old tannic tea. Towelless, I got out of the shower and, drenched, made it back into my dorm room where, slowly, with great effort, I found fresh underwear, and put on a new set of blue jeans. I rolled the towel through my soaked hair, then took out a new teeshirt from my clothes closet. I was still damp, but now it smelled simply like blue jeans, the student bathroom was stuck to me as an odor that felt neutral, institutional.

I then fumbled through my dimly-lit dorm room, to find something, anything, that might be used to shred and cut my hair now. I found the pack of Gillette razor blades, refills for when I shaved my underarms and legs, in the top drawer with my underthings. I pulled the pack out. I slowly slipped one of the blades out of the thick paper wrapping, and then I went to the bed and, sitting on the edge, I slashed a razor across my wrist. The blood was so slight, I hardly saw it, or felt it, but there I was cut and aching for relief, which momentarily, seeing some blood gather at the heel of my hand, allowed me to breathe out a long wind of release. Then I told myself I could not stay here in the remains of the night any longer.

I threw on a parka and rushed out the dormitory doors. Outside, another light November sleet was smacking the lawn near my dorm. The college campus appeared dark and empty. No one would be walking in this dark. I had to try to find Faith and tell her what happened. There was still some hope; it was what she made me feel and it quelled the other self.

I had left my dorm room at nine o'clock by the clock on my dresser, but by the gloom outside, it seemed later.

Sleet was brushing through the cold air, but now I was bundled in my parka. My sleepiness made the campus feel wet, and uncertain. I travelled up the steps at Westlands and then through the main lawn, where the volleyball net was glistening with fresh sleet. I followed the driveway up to Andrews, and even from a distance, I could see the lights on where Faith's office was. I was surprised to find my feet moving as I was headlong bent for Faith's office. I pushed myself through a mass of prickly strawberry bushes, and the blood was throbbing in my ears. My wrist throbbed, and I had to see if I was still bleeding. I saw only a long scratch on my wrist. I hadn't realized until Faith came out of the building that

I was making a commotion, and I started swaying dizzily as soon as I saw her.

"What the hell is going on?" I heard Faith's alarmed voice, and soon Faith was beside me, covered only by her afghan and shivering. "It's cold as hell out here. What the hell?" Faith's face looked stricken, as if scared. And when I presented myself at last to her, all her muscles seemed to soften as fear left her face and she was staring at me.

"What's the matter? What happened? Did someone attack you? You're cockeyed to be out in this weather. Me, I'm only stalling because I'm deathly afraid of the highway and didn't want to risk the damn Hudson River Parkway or whatever it's called. Honey, I have to ask because I can smell you. I have nose powers but that's a whole story. I just have a sense that you've had some alcohol?"

"I'm sorry," I said.

"Don't be sorry. That's a silly thing to be in a predicament such as this. You're out in the godforsaken sleet. And were you running? Is someone chasing you? I can call the campus guard you know. Are you hurt, Sweetheart?" Faith asked.

The darkness made shadows, and we made quite a pair, Faith and me. Opposites — me, the thin defeated, pissing, nothing of a girl who cut herself and then the buxom motherly, popular, and famous woman, undaunted, open-armed. "Let's go inside. Let's go to my office and talk this out. I want to know everything. Come, Cookie, come inside."

I was finally back in the room I had loved so much, in the same position on the floor as I had been before, but I thought I could still smell that urine wetness on myself, which lingered despite my shower, and I began to shake, wrapping both arms in a hold across my own chest.

"What? What?" Faith asked, kneeling beside me. "Tell me."

"Something happened with Dickers. . ."

"He's that much of a bastard? I underestimated."

"We had sex."

"Yeah, I figured."

"The story is a terrible story." It was calming, Faith's wide eyes holding me.

"Bastard!" Faith stood. "Wait," she said, and suddenly whisked herself out the office door, "Just sit there and wait," she said before she let the office's door shut behind her as she raced somewhere I couldn't imagine, though I knew Faith was not deserting me there. I was confused but oddly calmed, and I pulled at the sleet-wet strands of my hair and didn't so much cry as heave breaths of relief out of my throat.

Faith burst back into the room with two large towels.

"Here, Sweetheart. No, sit, stay and sit. Just dry up and we'll talk. We'll talk forever if that will help. I want you to tell me."

I took the towels and rubbed my head with one as the other sat in my lap, and each felt good and warm.

"It's a story you need to tell right now," Faith said. "Or I will be very worried he got inside you in all kinds of other bad ways that men do, that bastard."

"Oh, Faith. . ." I started.

"Did you fuck?"

"Yes."

"What kind of fucking? I'm asking, and please answer me fast, did he force you?"

"No, it wasn't like that exactly."

"Well, thank God. Wait —" Faith went to her desk and came back with a brush in her hand. "Shush now. Let me see." Faith touched my head with the flat of her left hand as her right hand was holding the brush. "Put the towel through it again sweetheart then I'll brush it, make it look like something new."

I took off my parka, pulling up my sweater sleeve and exposing the cut on my wrist.

"Oh, no," was all Faith said, staring at the dried blood.

"No," I said, pulling the towel through my hair one more time, and then pulling my sweater down to cover the wrist's cut. "You don't understand."

"What? What don't I understand, sweetheart?" Faith asked, starting to brush out my hair. "You have lovely hair, honey. Look, you fucked a guy you shouldn't have. I was so wild with the boys, my mother almost threw me out of her house. She died before I could make it up to her. Stone dead, my mother." She paused, caught for a brief moment in her own storytelling. "If you're not going to tell, I'll tell you. I understand being crazy for boys, men. This I grasp like the handle of this fucking brush. Hold still." She pulled the brush again across my head and my hair felt straightened out, as if by a wave.

"I drank before I let him touch me."

"Yeah? I get that. I can smell it on you. It's bad. Not the fucking, these things happen to a young woman, but the drinking."

Suddenly Faith put down the brush and grabbed me up into her arms. And held me so that I could smell Faith's soft skin, and her breath that smelled like bread.

"I think I wet myself on him," I finally said as everything began to feel surreal. "I urinated on him."

Even in this chapel of maternity, I was scared again after I let this out. "He's too fucking much for you," Faith said after a long breathy pause, "I'm upset too. This upsets me in a big way. It's women saving women

101

in a woman-hating world of men," she said. "Are you sure that was pee, sweetheart? Women get wet there. All the time they get wet there."

I, confused by this thought, sat up. My hair, brushed and a little dryer, felt like a warm wool hat. I stood up.

"Wait, I'm calling the school." Faith reached for the black receiver of the phone on her desk.

"No, no! I did it willingly."

Faith lay down the receiver. "They owe me good, this principal or important person, I'll tell them in the morning, you're coming to my class. I didn't show up for a few functions, so they're a little angry at me. But I still will try to make them listen to me."

"I have to go," I said, quickly.

"No, no, you are only temporarily fucked up." Faith said. "Do you want to sleep here tonight maybe? There are some pillows and a blanket in the closet near the kitchen."

"Mrs. Hale —"

"Faith, Cookie. I'll get some blankets. I have to get some sleep too. You stay there and I'll go by the window with my blanket when I get it, and we'll sleep here together and figure it out in the morning. I had a fight with my husband, Don. I came up to the college to do some work, but now I see you and we could both use some sleep." Faith shook her head. Then she headed out the door, returning a few minutes later with an armful of blankets and two pillows, and looking like she was losing her balance;, the first pillow was nearly in her eyes. But when she came back, she started to cough, as if she had contracted a cold. I, made more aware now, saw that Faith's face was pale as a sheet of paper. Was she sick?

"Faith," I said.

"No, I'm not sick. Don't pay attention." Faith said quickly, but I could sense with alarm that Faith had not been well.

I said nothing more, but helped Faith, motioning to her to let me carry some of the load.

"Take that blanket and lie down, and here," Faith knocked her forehead against the pillows over the blanket in her arms, "take one of these pillows too."

Carefully, as if I were a diver picking up precious stones from the floor of the sea, I held my breath and took one blanket and one pillow. Now Faith's face was visible again, and her smile. "Good, good. OK, watch your legs," Faith said while in one muscular heave she spread out her blanket on the floor and motioned to me to spread out my blanket next to hers.

"It's simple arithmetic," Faith suddenly said. "At least one of the men teaching here had to turn out to be a rat. You dry enough now, Pussycat?"

I nodded slowly, because I wasn't sure I was dry at all, except for my hair, which Faith had so lovingly brushed. But staring down at the two blankets strewn now on the floor, I realized Faith expected me to lie beside her, and the warmth of the room was so overpowering it began to make me dizzy.

"Mrs. Hale —"

"Faith."

"Faith. What am I going to do?" The hazy tenderness of a mass of loose, long hair was near me now. Faith was asking me to lie down beside her. Faith's tenderness almost blinded me, but Faith motioned to me to lay my body flat out on the floor under her blanket. I let myself stretch out as Faith settled the blanket on top of us both and herself right next to me. And then — I was lost in her.

"I wasn't so fat then, when I was running around with boys, but heavier in the muscles I would say. I always disappointed my ma and papa, you might say, running around with boys, on the neighborhood porches chatting with my friends when I should have been in school. So one day they decided, I swear to you, they would kick me out of said school. And it was my sister Jeannette who came to plead my case to the big director at NYU College. Sisters have always been important to me. Mothers, too busy or sick. Fathers, too in love with their own voices and ideas. I had friends who had to have abortions when it was not legal. You have written an important piece of writing, Allegra. This praise I pass on to you like a garment, a dress from the famous store of hard luck. Sisters you can call friends and vice versa will be your salvation. Think of me that way, darling. It's why I'm here with you now." There was only a sliver of light left in the room from the window and the moon, as Faith had first shut off her desk lamp to stop talking.

"Give it some hours — get some sleep," Faith said. "He won't get in you again. None of that dirty stuff is going to kill you anyway, sweetheart. I couldn't even tell my mother all I had done with boys."

Then Faith burst out: "Whatever more you want to tell me, you can tell me later when you are more OK. I understand. I understand what happened. I will not say it to anyone."

And I thought — this is the end of my story. I am with Faith Hale now. It is safe and pure. I am finally saved, and this is the end at last.

But less than an hour later, after I thought Faith was asleep, I heard and felt Faith start coughing. It wasn't so much a loud coldish, cough but like a cigarette cough, though I knew Faith didn't smoke. Getting up to go to the bathroom to find a washcloth to wipe Faith's brow that was sweating, and her neck, too, and whatever of her side and back I saw also dotted with sweat beads,

I walked past the classroom and into the tiny, chestnut-wood bathroom with tiles of sailboats on the floor.

Faith was sweating heavily in her sleep when I slipped back into the room, and I didn't want to wake her, though I was afraid — but then I rationalized, wasn't the room just too hot? With the blankets, and the weight of words they had carried? No, everything was fine, Faith was fine, I told myself.

And before it all fell apart, there was this dream that night with Faith lying beside me.

I dreamed I was urinating and everything was just right, the hot flow between my thighs, no longer disgusting and foul or a dirty piece of me. And then I saw a lake. It was oblong like a large glistening table top. Suddenly, I grabbed a rope from the sky, and holding onto it like a child blissful at play, I flew over the lake holding the rope. . .I flew — I flew, I remembered, and I was happy — not that evanescent drunken kind of happiness, but happy.

It was two weeks later, after I had visited Faith three times more in her office during the day, that I found Faith Hale's story about me in the latest *Ms.* magazine. The facts had been changed, but that was it, my story.

"Woman's Body, Woman's Mind" was the title of the whole section. The small print read: "The Women's Movement and our heightened awareness that has been denied knowledge and control, our bodies determined by male doctors. This has, nonetheless produced a desire to learn about our bodies and our sexuality." And then there was the story, by Faith Hale, entitled "Lena, the Lost Girl." In the story, an older woman very much like Faith had felt soft and protective toward a confused young college girl with dark hair, a former actress in bit roles on television soap operas. The girl is taken advantage of by an older male famous author, nearly raped. The girl loses control and urinates on the man and then, later, cuts her wrist. In the same issue, there were clinical descriptions of how a woman can also just "wet" when she orgasms, and Faith's story was meant to show the naked dangers of one's own vagina going out of control, as well as the power inherent in an adopted matriarchy to help such a person. Segments of Adrienne Rich's quotes on the power of matriarchy were spread like gathered thoughts throughout the article. Faith had prefaced it: "so many of these girls come to me, and this girl had beautiful brown eyes." The girl in the story cuts the skin on her wrist with a razor, and had had an abortion months before the man sexed her, but then I read more, then all of it.

At first, I felt a headache pinch at my temples, my fingers went to rub my hairline, as if suddenly overwhelmed by fever. It was humiliation and rage rising up from my bowels. I had been betrayed; Faith Hale had written about me and betrayed me and there was no other feeling I could ever remember as painful. Whatever had happened was all for the "Women's Movement," like the book I read in the library. I realized this with pain and consternation and some hate. The anger simmered down to a persistent ache, as if my mind had been affected with rickets. She had been using me, I told myself bitterly, I was one of her many sycophants and followers. I was shaking now, and then crying, and then staggering. Faith Hale had written about me without restraint or guilt, feeling not a bit of responsibility to me. I threw the story on the desk without thinking and I ran from the story and from my love of Faith Hale. The whole world would know of my shame. I ran from what felt like a shot to my heart and I ran toward the river.

When I got to the trees and bank, I followed a stairway of leaves laid on the ground to the river's edge and then picked up three large and heavy stones, stashing them inside my parka. And then I jumped into the water, sinking. Seconds later, in sudden panic, I pushed the stones out and floated up. Do it, I told myself, but instead pulled myself to the bank of iced leaves and thin snow. Without any more thinking, then as if I had been dying already and it would do no good to stay ashore, I pushed myself back into the muddy water. If I could drown and kill myself and die, I would awaken to a radiant array of stars, I thought, to the other side of life, vibrant with light, and my father, at long last would be there, I thought. Surely an incandescence would come and cancel out this horrible betrayal by Faith, I would be embraced by a great white light and out of this life. The climax was certainly soon to be replaced by pure stars. I would be free of any more emotional soaring or violent plunges. The water rushed in and pumped against my cheeks. I started choking on it — it was filled with twigs and leaf bits and mud. It tasted like a dead animal. But then, I felt a sudden terror and my body in a new fight — it started to surface, not drown, peddling and speeding upward until there was a cold pounding at my face and I had surfaced, alive. I had the vision of the woman octopus on the *Ms.* magazine in my head in the fuzzy, mental journey upwards. But the octopus was a woman in my fantasy, and she was naked and wildly crazy and hopeless as the octopus cruelly chased her in the water. Very slowly, I finally pulled myself out of the river, standing on the bank, having saved myself from drowning. My hair must have been almost black with mud, and I was shivering so hard when I heard a voice call. I looked to see a boy on the bridge shout and call down to me. "Did you fall in? What happened?" I must have looked sopped and soaked and desperate, because he trudged down the bank to me, and I looked at him and just started crying and then I told him I had tried to kill myself. I couldn't tell him what happened. I had meant to tell him the whole tale, but I couldn't stop sobbing. "You could catch pneumonia," he said softly, "Easy now, let's call for some help." He was big and blond and gentle, and I thought I had imagined him later. Who could be so kind as to call an ambulance for such a stupid girl in her aborted suicide attempt? But he existed, and I soon found myself in the back of an ambulance, alone, in blankets, wrapped like a child. "I wanted to die," I said to the nurse beside me.

Chapter Seven.

The ambulance arrived at New York Hospital in White Plains at around five o'clock and I was still thinking of Faith. I was then inside an elegant Tudor building filled with antique nineteenth century-like rugs, chestnut armoires, a grandfather clock, and mahogany tables with lamps shaped like Aladdin's lanterns, also antique, 1930s. I didn't know exactly the date, but there was something Hollywood about the beautiful building and interior, its polished perfection and stillness. One expected Joan Crawford or Bette Davis to emerge from inside their hollow halls, crazy but with perfect hairdos, in a lavish setting like one imagines from the old-time movie "asylums." It had been Faith, though, the obverse reflection of such glamour, who had emerged again in my desire and imagination, in my regret and hurt. The imprint was going to dissolve, I was thinking. I was lost now to madness.

The sparse, institutional ward for women was different from the rest of the estate, with netting-guarded windows and a nursing station, bright and fluorescent-lit. They ushered me in, cold and shivering and wet, and by that time, they had asked if I had meant to end my life. I didn't answer. All I remembered was the door opening, and suddenly the sunlight on the carpets departing as a dark ward replaced the outside hallway under my feet, and the sun from the window was like the last breath of warmth and understanding I would know for the rest of my life.

It was to Hall Eight North, an all-women ward that I had been ushered into. I was led by a nurse to a young-ish doctor who was writing vigorously away on a sheet of paper. I only remembered a tiny bit of the admitting interview with the sterile doctor. "Do you know who the current president is?" "I'm going to give you five num-bers and ask you to recite them backward to me." "I'm going to ask you to remember five words and then I'll ask you to repeat them back to me." "What dooes 'people who live in glass houses shouldn't throw stones mean'" "Who are you?" "What issues would you say brought you here?"

Dr. Zorn, a very young woman in a silky skirt, wear-ing black stockings and Liz Claiborne pumps the color of radishes, was assigned to me. Dr. Zorn's hair was long and shiny, black as coal. She was a slender woman of low height carrying a pretty, brown-eyed face. Dr. Zorn could have been a senior at college; her age seemed slippery so one could not quite pin it down, but I later learned she was twenty-nine from one of the nurses. Dr. Zorn had already done her internship at McLean, a leading psychiatric hospital, the Harvard of booby hatches. She shopped for her clothes with attention to terrific style: a neat, orderly but beautiful array of dresses and skirts to her thin calves, and blouses such as a New York model might wear — not florid but plain and perfectly ironed and neat, with faint colors like a faded blue or spank-ing-clean white. She could have been anyone walking a street in Manhattan of whom I might think, what an attractive woman. She came to this ward of weary women with those outfits, to women feeling only their own tat-ters — Dr. Zorn seemingly oblivious to what the women would feel at all. She had been maddeningly perfect, a model of a sprite, bright and clever student who, when she held the hall keys, looked out of her depth standing in the ward. The only vulnerable part of Dr. Zorn seemed illustrated by the no smoking signs all over her office. She might be afraid of cigarette smoke even if she wasn't afraid of mental patients.

I wouldn't take calls from Faith. Not even after I had been here three weeks on "close watch" and on a drug called Thorazine.

One afternoon in the hospital ward, someone called down: "Allegra, isn't this her?" And I rushed to see Faith Hale on television. It was *The Dick Cavett Show*, her hair was up like a layer of cake on top of her large head. "My guest has found herself in a very particular situation," Dick Cavett seemed to croon. "She's been arrested by the United States government for stepping on the White House lawn with a 'ban the bombs banner.' What can you tell us about this, Mrs. Hale? We know you for your short stories but very little about your political activism —"

I ran out of the room, holding my face in my hands, and an aide stopped me. "Did you know that woman on TV?" she asked.

When Faith tried to contact me on the patient phone in the hallway, the number they must have given her when she called the hospital, someone would call out "Allegra! Faith Hale is on the phone again," but I wouldn't come, throwing up my arms and hands to signal the messenger to hang up on her. Faith kept trying. How did Faith hear about what happened? I wondered. And does everyone at Abigail Stone know I'm in a mental hospital? Did everyone know I was the girl in Faith's story? Hadn't Faith identified me by saying I was the girl who had been in the soap opera? It was a fact I shared liberally at the college to strangers to make myself important. Had it been predictable that the dark states would return? Without Faith or the hope of Faith's imprint, the illness appeared naked of hope, and it grew deeper.

I called Sofia the first day, and she had started crying on the phone, but they did not let her visit me for fear her presence would make it all worse. I told Dr. Zorn about the darkness, which made me want to tailor a blue-jean noose, the constant calling to death from my father, and the "white light."

Dr. Zorn kept me on suicide watch.

If tedium and boredom were fatal diseases, I would have died those first weeks in the hospital.

Whenever I sat in the hall amid the throng of women patients, I kept thinking of the patients like the neutrinos who, as Dickers had attempted to explain, had populated the atmosphere since the 1960s. "The neutrino is especially fascinating, Allegra." He told me, "Neutrinos are created as a result of certain types of radioactive decay, or nuclear reactions. Did you know they do not feel the electromagnetic force?" For the dulled, sometimes beaten and confused faces I saw around me, I imagined the world of the changing social forces in the country and its atmosphere could not be felt by them, that these women had been left behind or expelled from the "new" world for not working properly like the feminist texts in the library instructed, and not being up to the task. They were mostly housewives and younger unmarried women, none of whom seemed remotely "crazy."

One day in the lounge, a woman patient named Dory was in a chair close to the dining room hallway — the androgynous Dory.

Dory had a boy's pixie haircut, which she summoned the only real "designer" hairdresser in the institution to trim, and the hairdresser gave her dirty brown hair some bangs, which Dory protested and moaned about almost everyday. Dory's bangs were straight as a broom's end, which made the rest of Dory's hair look sort of straw-like, too. This tailored boys haircut covered half her ears, leaving her lobes visible, like little lumps of flesh, or shards disembodied from the rest of her head. Would I look like that soon, I thought. Dory's clothes, too, were boyish, masculine — a short-sleeved, finely ironed, blinding-white dress shirt, the kind boys wear to church any Sunday. She looked like a spruced up private school student wearing her best perfectly creased trousers and shirt, but her shoes were Norwegian clogs, and under them she wore thick white gym socks. Her manners — highly cultivated, with explosive rage boiling behind her careful sentences — were just like my own. As if Dory were saying, and I could say the same, "Yes, Professors, I know I am to take the geography exam today. . . but there seems to be something wrong with my writing hand because every knuckle, every fiber on it wants to murder you. And to leave you for dead on the doorstep of your fucking women's ward, to suffer the indignities of being locked up with these murderous hospital rules and restrictions like we do." Dory looked how I felt. Dory and her past were a reminder of how severe it could get if I didn't vanquish the dark states forever, or at least figure out how to make them release me back into a world of less danger. I was feeling that there was no Faith, or hope of returning to Faith. And feeling a public humiliation because of Faith that I would never live down. I couldn't even bear seeing her on television that one day.

The Thorazine made me hungry. I loaded up on snacks from a machine which I called the "white machine." Yesterday, Dory told me about the other hospital, Columbia Presbyterian, called "PI" — in short, a psychiatric institution near the Bronx.

"We lived in only our pajamas with no hall privileges, and because we were permitted no privacy, they watched all of us," Dory had explained to me. "You had to ask permission to get a drink of water from the fountain or pee. Patients, wall to wall, imprisoned in their nightclothes, crying, and chewing their hair, which only made it worse for them; some hadn't been dressed for days, some for weeks." Dory was moved to this Westchester Division of Cornell for insubordination at PI. I was sure that the punishment of wearing pajamas at all hours was not strong enough to keep Dory from trying to commit suicide again. But the threat was enough for me to watch myself. Four weeks into PI, Dory had tried to get out a window and was caught just in the nick of time before she fell three stories to her near death. It had landed her on serious suicide watch for weeks there at Columbia Presbyterian, and she instigated constant loud protests — getting the pajama-imprisoned patients to go on a hunger strike, and organizing a buck-naked protest in which all the patients took off their pajamas, put them in the center of the hall in a big, dirty pile, and lay around naked. When she was transferred to White Plains — "Bloomingdales" — Dory was less successful in organizing protests and could wear her street clothes, which the nurses kept referring to whenever she reared up and roared. A nurse would tell her, "This isn't prison though, is it Dory?" It was more a nursery, I thought to myself; we were infants, babies run by a relentless squad of mama-monsters. And the nurses would say: "We want only to protect you against yourself." I, along with a group of other patients, had witnessed Dory's last attempt with hung bedsheets. Dory had to rip the sheets off her bed to perform the act of attempted self-murder, but the nurses were always on to her plans. Still, I often thought they might get it wrong some day and Dory would procure a makeshift noose so secretly and cleverly, they would miss the cues. When they caught Dory and took her to the seclusion room, it haunted the hall for days.

One day, Dory looked up at me from an old *Time* magazine and asked, "You still on C.O.?"

"I am," I answered. "And the way it looks, I will be on it 'til the end of my days; I haven't been let off the hall."

Other patients were in the lounge now, too, a kaleidoscope of faces. Benedine, in her straw hat, all dressed up in a new yellow chiffon dress, was talking about the Brandy Alexanders she had when she was taken to the local tavern by a visitor, who had been an old friend but could not brave the sight of them all in this stifling restricted ward. And a nun in plain clothes now, chubby and problematic, who had grasped my hand the night before over snacks. "Do you understand? Do you understand?" She kept saying in desperate whispers, "I can only come in orgasm if I imagine a man whipping my backside with his belt. Only then."

Was it the previous day that Dr. Zorn came in the morning? The patient, Thelma, was lecturing anybody who would listen on the mystical primordial garden that we were back inside of because of our dysfunction in the outside society. Thelma's teeth were large as oystershells, her reddish-brown hair pinned back into a bun. "The patriarchy is evil," she said. "We are parched with evil, get it?"

And there were times, it was true, like that day, that I waited, almost counted the hours when Dr. Zorn would arrive and listen to what seemed like a private hum of doom that started in my groins and moved up through my throat into the indifferent air.

"Tell me," Dr. Zorn said as we sat on a cement bench at the edge of the well-kept forest. She had taken me off the ward, into the crisp outside.

"I never wanted to really kill myself," I said suddenly to Dr. Zorn, as if it was a confession in a novel.

"But you've told me you feel like you want to die often, " Dr. Zorn said, her tiny form against the wide and massive woods that stretched all the way to Bloomingdale's shopping district if one knew the correct path to run away on.

"Do you know what you call the darkness really is, Allegra?"

I did not want to ever use the words depression or suicide. I had my own words, I wanted to say. "Darkness" was my word. I didn't want to use her words.

"Tell me what is torturing you so," Dr. Zorn persisted.

"The darkness," I would answer again. It was easier after I told Dr. Zorn about the "black sun," which caused the "darkness." Later, I talked about my father and his Proust, the scent of him, like strawberries, about our love for each other, about the pull toward him, conscious, painful as a broken limb and then how he, my father, would never come back and how because of that I wanted to go with him into death. Sometimes I was him, I told her. Sometimes I was just like him. And then I told her all about Faith Hale. And how she wrote a story about a secret I told her. I barely spoke about the shameful pissing with Dickers and how I had run to Faith as if she were the "mother" that would correct the denigration that was my life. That would have stopped my father calling me into death and illness. But I didn't trust Dr. Zorn. My words were short and well-controlled.

"She said you had considerable talent as a writer," Dr. Zorn said.

"Who's 'she'? What 'she'?"

"Faith Hale called me. She told me a lot."

I felt the beginnings of a rage welling up from my stomach when I first heard this.

"Only because she thought it might help you," Dr. Zorn added quickly, but already I was fading into that numb state where I knew would soon fall into the darkness again.

"Mrs. Hale said she was certain no one would ever know she had been writing about you. She said she was sorry she used details, that she was wrong. 'What I did was dead wrong,' she said. Mrs. Hale has a tough voice, but I am deeply certain she cares for you very much."

"Then you know all that happened." I whispered. I'm a fool, I said to myself.

I first felt a kind of whimper, then a warning of flooding tears. I couldn't trust this pretty, well-dressed woman with those deer eyes to catch me crying. It would only make everything worse if I let the tears overtake me, and yet, I was stunned still by the sheer force of my tears trying to wash away my rage, as if to tell her, let me out, let me out. I won't fall into the darkness again; it will be different from before, if you let me out and let me see Faith again.

"Are you all right, Allegra?" I heard Dr. Zorn ask now, and I knew I had succeeded not to cry out loud, not visibly.

"Do you want to go back to the ward now?" Dr. Zorn then asked after a few seconds passed, as if she knew I had to get away from her at that point. The other parts to this drama could be played out, but slowly, cautiously, Dr. Zorn must have thought; she was a cautious woman. Having her in my head felt like pickles in brine.

The grounds of the hospital were elegantly laid out with walkways and gardens. I was spending most of my time in the center lounge, though with a "watcher." I had a green-backed spiral notebook I had bought when someone wheeled in a supply cart with things to buy on it: paperclips, rubber bands, paper, and other office-like supplies. I got two pencils and started to write about the hospital, my feelings, the other weird patients. "I've never seen such self-hatred," Dr. Zorn said once, quietly but attentively. I could taste the briny, sour consciousness of being in someone else's hands.

One night in the stuffy dorm, I had a dream about Dr. Zorn. She was holding me down under the water in the river near Abigail Stone College. She was thrusting my head down. I was breaking. Dr. Zorn pulled me up and I stared at the tiny, wiry woman. Then I felt for a moment we were going to make love. I lifted myself out of the water and stood. I felt Dr. Zorn's beautiful face come down to my lips and touch them, and then a hot flush seemed to transit through my flesh, then a horrible piercing pain, and then finally a reflexive unwanted spasm in my groin. Her body on mine was the death of all things. The imprint was dissolving, I told myself, and this fearful other place where the imprint had nestled was now opened up. It was like being shot with a gun. The sessions in Dr. Zorn's office became surreal, like bruises weeping honeyed tears deep underneath my skin, and I became spellbound within myself. I did not trust this woman and her beautiful outfits, her voice as clear as a rehearsed actress on a stage. It felt as if I was swallowing the force of an unseen enemy like a plundered lover, shuddering in shock. The spasm in my frightened sex remains like a tumor in remembrance, a cancer unbearable to remember. For tiny breaths of time Dr. Zorn was penetrating me. This was all that my vagina responded to then. But the Thorazine, sometimes a blessing. numbed and dampened the bodily reactions.

It was a hideous machine, the white machine. Tiny fluorescent lights shown on the cellophaned wraps of sandwiches and sweets. I went to it after the dreams, in the morning, drawn lemming-like to a cliff, the machine in the wall, with tubes that looked like plumbing which fastened it to the hospital wall. I was seduced, not hungry, and because of this often found myself in tears, falling to the floor sometimes, in an orgy of oblivion. I would fall to the floor until the tears became a convulsing belly cry for help. Once Sheldon, an aide, found me on the floor, my lips smeared with chocolate and mayonnaise. I only stopped the visits to the machine, the pulling of levers, the shameful gorging, when I ran out of coins. I had no hunger for anything else; this was real madness I thought, the housed stale sandwiches, and I had no body now except for the protrusions from the machine. My jeans could hardly be pulled up and on anymore; I wore only a hospital gown in this daze, which only made me cry at doorways and in front of the nurses station.

"The white machine has unearthed me," I wrote in my notebooks. Exhaustion and grief inched heavily into every fiber of my body, yet I was wide awake. My stomach braided up to my throat.

I visited this candy machine, the white machine, often. I found I could walk to it when I got escorted for brief passes with a watcher from the hall. I wrote one night from my bed, "In the white machine is the worst candy: stale M&M's, Mars bars where the chocolate is so dated and old, it cracks like plastic in your hands. And there are these terrible bologna sandwiches on stale white bread. All I want to do is be near this white machine and put coins in that white machine and fill myself with the horrible treats forever, numbing me to any other life."

Chapter Eight.

"I cannot feel my genitals," I wrote in my notebook one morning. "Now I watch the heart of the outside sky through the locked windows. I have been here two months." I still wasn't accepting calls from Faith.

"I am piss," I told Dr. Zorn the previous afternoon. "But I have this imprint," I continued after a silence had passed between us, "and it makes me no longer feel like piss. I'm sorry you don't understand a fucking thing about it. It will save me — this imprint — if I forgive Faith for what she's done. It's an impossible impasse. I cannot bring myself to forgive her."

"Tell me more about Faith and what she's done to you." Dr. Zorn had said, settling back in her desk chair, clearly uncomfortable in one of her outfits, which seemed to shine. I thought I heard the rip of Zorn's fashionable skirt, and almost felt delighted out loud from it. But then she sat still, unripped, untouched.

"Is the imprint about Faith Hale?" She had asked after a few seconds went by, though not for the first time. "Often patients form an idealization of someone, a mother figure, and it's strong. But it isn't an imprint exactly, Allegra. They call it that in small animals. Though it can be very, very helpful."

"Never mind," I said.

"Allegra, Faith cares about you, but she's not your mother, and you have to face that you never had the mother you wanted. And that you will be facing this illness for years to come. There might even be more hospitalizations. We have hard work to do here. And I think I will be the one that helps. We need to talk about your real mother and you, your feelings about your real mother, and me. " Dr. Zorn said.

"No, I never felt that," I said, absentmindedly, because I wasn't listening or responding to anything else she said. I had closed my mind by then in distrust.

Now, in the center lounge, behind locked doors a nurse was giving a condescending report of the day outside to the staff assembled in the dining room. Down the hall, someone had turned off the incessant TV. I wanted to turn myself off as well, too agitated to entrust myself to the open spaces of this closed ward, with its possibilities of haphazard, impersonal encounters in the hall. I was thrashing in my bed-sheets during our daytime rest time, loosening the sheets and creasing them.

One cold night I had dreamed I took Faith Hale down to the river by Pondfield Road and we sat where I had drank my Macallan's, peering into the long stream of water going south to New York City. And in the dream, I was telling Faith everything, how Dickers had finally touched my breasts and ordered me to undress, how I only did it to get into Faith's class, how I might have done it because I had been drinking and suddenly let go, and then I had been pissing on him and it made me feel ashamed. Then I was asking, "How could you betray me, Faith?" We were having a long conversation,

and Faith told me we were going into New York City by
a train that would come soon. And everything would be
all right again.

As I had grown used to, it was just another morning that I was forced to sit in the busy patient lounge
after the usual breakfast of fried eggs on rye toast
with hotel-like butter dabs wrapped up like chewing gum. In the half an hour before breakfast while
dressing, combing my lifeless hair, and preparing for
another day of idleness, inactivity, and visits to the
white machine, I had worried about how fat I was.

There were six beds in each dorm, and for some
reason I couldn't fathom how the room always smelled
like newly washed cars. They moved me there when a
new girl came and needed my private room. Old bureaus
were against the wall in the dorm where clothes had
been randomly thrown in drawers, mostly half-opened,
as were the lives those patients had been thrown in, too.
The nurses' station was only a few feet outside, and the
two doors were never closed. Though, except for after ten
in the evening, the lights were on, and there was only
a grayish tint to everything as if there were downcast
rainclouds hovering around the ceiling, about to burst.

I started writing in my notebook about the other
patients when I moved to the dorms. In the dorm room,
a bed apart from me, a fat girl, Diedre, had a face which
ran into itself. She lay under the covers of her steel-
framed bed, her thumb always seemed to be wandering
under her face, as if it would, in a split second of desire
overtake her, push into her mouth so she could suck it.
Her face was pimpled; her overweight self gave a picture
of her body as limp and saggy and fat. Her face looked
like a middle-aged man; if not for two small breasts
under her man-tailored blue shirts, I would have taken
her for a boy. When she got up, it was to go to breakfast,

lunch, or dinner, soon to return to her bed, where she lay forgetting to take her black lace-up sneakers off, and the nurses would come over, their words meant to both calm and contain her. I overheard, "Now, Diedre, it isn't like that," or "Dear, you have to get out of here sometime," meant to answer Diedre's plaintive cries that she was unable to move or speak, which underlined the unsaid words that she thought herself ugly and ungainly, like some kind of horse who couldn't make it in the stables of life, where, she was sure, other people wanted her to prance around with confidence. She called out "Mama!" late at night, and then I would hear a fleet of nurses flee to her side, ready with orange juice or a glass of milk, adjusting her blankets. Diedre, kept as a baby and catered to by those I continued to call in my notebook the "mama-monsters," those aides and nurses who piled into the dormitory to subdue and soothe us all — nurses who with their whispery voices managed to cover most of the cliches frequently used on mental patients. The mama-monsters would say "There's always tomorrow," and the phrase that made me cringe each time I heard it "You will feel differently when you get better."

I soon realized I was writing about Diedre, other patients, and the ward to show Faith one day — or was it because I was fighting against the fear that I might turn into one of them soon? I told myself Faith and I would again be together, and my writing would be even stronger. I was learning so much about character and story. Faith Hale had called the ward for me so many times, and I still would not speak to her. It would have to be a while for us to be together again. The thought of her still made me only want to go to the white Machine now.

In the gloom of many days, I often lay on my cot in the dorms, or sat in the center lounge with my notebook and pencil. I wrote about the almost-drowning in the river and about the blond boy. Then I wrote again at last about my father.

"I saw his clothes in some kind of butcher's paper," I wrote, "I was sure they were packing up his remains as I stood, sequestered by my mother, in the house by the sea. There were gigantic, wide windows outward in that house, enabling me to look outward. They made such an assembly, my mother and the police, and the strangers packing up my father for the morgue. . ."

One morning, as I looked around the center lounge, the aide, Sheldon, put a marker between the pages in the novel she was reading, *Watership Down*. A nursing student was staring dumbly at the small wobbly table where the snacks were usually placed each day after 8:00 pm. The staff wouldn't be out of the dining room for another hour, I was figuring, and I had Sheldon and this nursing student with me on "close watch" until dinner time. What could I do but check whatever mirror would be on the wall when they took me for walks?

In the bathroom of Hall Eight every morning before breakfast, I would check that everything was in place on me. I would look down: vagina still there despite all my absence of feelings. I would announce to myself, breasts and feet present! They seemed to chime in, yet inside my brain was only a great nullity, a vacancy, even naked, after I undressed for the shower where one of the aides would watch, the water rolling off my numbed flesh.

Usually, I shuffled through drying, returning to my dorm room for yet another pair of blue jeans to be pulled on. By then I would be on my third cigarette and the lights would all be on, the eight o'clock morning nursing staff arriving while I would be planning how to get to the white machine. Weeks of this inertia and stupefaction passed so slowly — hardly at all it seemed. It was a melting into the white machine life, what I called the nurture-nurture labyrinth in my notebook. Faces of nurses, younger students, the seeming endlessness ma-ma-monsters, and the weight of it all. I did not try to kill myself. It seemed enough just to vanish into an oblivion full of pain. Time was slow, always agonizing, but the days sped by in a disorderly mass of habits and customs. The sessions with Dr. Zorn hardly grew deeper. Subjects of Sofia, of my father, like colored crayons in a child's art set, drawn large but shallow. Dr. Zorn, in her fashion-able clothes, was like a punishment, a humiliation, but I knew if I ever wanted to go home again, we would have to talk about something.

There was a plain metal-framed bed in my dorm room for me, and a worn white bedspread, more like a tablecloth. Then a dingy mirror. Clean-ing, Windexing it, wouldn't get the dinginess out. Streaks and smudges, a trail of cleaning, purpose-ful hands working on it the way they work on the thoughts inside my head. Just leaving streaks and smudges. I still couldn't look in it and recognize the image as myself. Wearing the same blue jeans everyday, washed in the laundry room, and feeling bloated from the Thorazine, the dorm room was the only room that smelled of something normal and recognizable. In the dusty mirror in the middle of the room, I saw my father's face in my own. We were both trapped now in madness.

Suddenly in the center lounge, I heard: "You're fuck-ing crazy, crazy, crazy." Someone was teasing one of the women who was in the same nightgown for two weeks and smelled of skin baked into sweat and dried tears, the body she thought was doomed — as all the patients who couldn't perform the days' activities smelled that one way. Ordinary skin and flesh became a wasteland of unwashed flesh and body fluids in that hospital. It was the secret language of mental illness — the alien, inhuman way people smelled dirty and guilty and unkempt. Even the housewives who came in were put on antidepressants that made them forget to brush their teeth because they became so euphorically relieved of any more responsibility of having to keep their houses and bodies clean. Others sometimes used their manic moods to order brand new clothes from Bloomingdale's. When their own dark states had come seizing them, some women started singing songs by rote from Broadway musicals that they suddenly remembered as their moods peaked to new heights of oblivion. "I feel pretty, oh, so pretty, I feel pretty, and witty and wise, "old Mrs. Morgan from Scarsdale sang for the morning visitors. "Oh, that's cute," Mrs. Forster, a manic depressive, would say whenever I started crying, because I simply felt lost in this community of women.

What I feared the most were my dreams of Dr. Zorn. In my notebook, I had written about these dreams. Was the imprint being replaced by this disciplined, small woman, and if so, would I also be a resident of some kind of other madness forever?

Now I was anxiously looking all around the room to see if one of the "nice" nurses was around, maybe Margo with her hefty, friendly body that felt protective as one's imagined and heavily idealized images of a big sister, would see me sweating and come to talk to me. The good nurses were, in contrast to the mama-monsters, the mama-wonders, and Margo was one of those. There was a girl named Judy Cohen, too, sitting Indian-style on the carpet listening to the other popular daytime nurse, Veronica, perhaps explaining to her that her mother's visit wouldn't be so obliterating this time, so Judy wouldn't have to be carted off again to the seclusion room tonight, screaming.

"Allegra Gordon, phone call!" I suddenly heard. It was someone calling for me from down the hallway. And just as suddenly, as if it were simply time after two months, I stood to walk the few yards to the public phone out in the middle of the hall. Sheldon shifted in her seat, then nodded at me.

"Allegra," Seconds later, on the phone, I recognized the voice of Faith Hale coming to me from the outside world like a blowhorn. "Allegra, honey, I fucked up. It's me. I didn't tell them who I was this time so you would come to the phone."

"Why do you keep calling me? Why?" I heard the bitterness in my own voice and I felt myself pulling back, sucking in my chest and breath.

"I've been calling for days. Weeks, even. Months, you can say now. Do they not give you messages at this place? As soon as I heard, I called the hospital and spoke to that woman therapist about you."

"They had no right, no right at all to tell you where I was."

"Was it about the story I wrote for *Ms.*? Because if it was about my story, I want you to know I know I fucked up bad. I really fucked up bad."

"You don't care about me," I didn't know where that had come from, it was from another part of me.

"No, no, sweetheart. I just fucked up. That's all."

Where was my voice coming from? I asked myself again. It was a soft voice, from which the rage had finally softened those many weeks, but had not been completely silenced. It was like the voice of a woman who had made love to a man then heard he spread rumors of her all over God's world.

"I will be missing two rallies this week because I couldn't sleep or eat, I couldn't let myself sleep." Faith said now.

Whoever was on the phone with me wasn't the same Faith Hale I knew, and like the hospital ward, with its stuffed rooms full of patients, nothing seemed quite real suddenly.

Faith sounded so different, shaken, and she was coughing again.

"Are you sick?" I asked, but Faith didn't answer.

"I'm so sorry," Faith said, like a drunk who had woken up from a night of behavior. "It was wrong of me to publish that story. You were so interesting, Allegra. If I could, I would take it all back."

"What's wrong with you?" I said, but loud, as if a scream.

"Let me come there, darling," Faith said.

"The ward doesn't allow visitors," I lied.

"My husband said to me, 'You really fucked up, Faithie, writing that story about that girl.'"

"Everyone knows."

"I see the courage in you," Faith said suddenly.

"I have to let someone use the phone, now." I said, hollowly.

"OK pussycat, OK. But I know I fucked up bad."

"Time's up," It was Sheldon, tapping me on the shoulder. She had moved from her seat in the center lounge to the phone and was motioning to me to hang up the phone.

"Faith —" I started, my voice softened.

"Yes, pussycat, yes —"

"They're making me get off now."

I let the receiver slip from my hand into the cradle, then Faith and her voice were gone.

In the lounge a few minutes after the call from Faith, Thelma was already dressed and smelled of some kind of Southern body wash, a black licorice scent. "Look at you, little Allegra, pretty thing," Thelma said to me. "If they were going to do a mental patient ad for TV, they'd have you on it, perfect figure, dark, big eyes like Natalie Wood. . ."

"What's going to be on the snack plate tonight?" would be the only bellow in the hall I knew, not thinking of Faith for a few relieved moments, and then lots of laconic discussions about their therapists hairstyles and clothes, and if the afternoon passed fast enough with its pointless outside games of volleyball and a walk to the formal gardens, everyone could get their second dose of meds and sit in the evening analyzing the day that hadn't so much passed as looped along, pulling them to another activity, another session, yet another new burst of tears and remorse, and then to the comforts of the eleven o'clock snack tray again like the white machine with the opened jar of peanut butter that might have been and should have been a vase of hope and comfort, a soothing invective to get better so they could eat again, so that one day soon they could be, exist, again. And then, by then I told myself, I could forget Faith called and that I spoke to her. Fall into hospital routine again. Would that save me, or Dr. Zorn? Or was it the routine and the hospital life itself that was killing me finally? Was Faith's phone call going to change anything? Was I going to get out of here and not become one of them?

"You a writer?" Thelma asked me now. "Because I always see you with that notebook."

"Faith Hale gave it me," I whispered, suddenly realizing how excited and relieved I was that Faith had called and that I just lied. But then suddenly realized, yes, I would call Faith back. Yes, I can do it, remembering Faith's plaintive remorse that had almost made her voice hoarse.

"No! No bologna, really?"

"Yes, the writer. Faith Hale."

"I sure do know who she is."

"She was my friend at school."

"Well, pinch me twice," Thelma said. "And I bet the pretty little thing you are, she's got her eye on you." I loved this Southern woman who could speak as poetically as the stars sometimes. Though she had a Southern drawl.

"No, no, it's not like that." I protested. "And I'm not so sure she's my friend now. We used to talk about so many things."

"We have to get out of here! We have to get out! How are we all going to teach these men and change the male/female duality so that the patriarchy doesn't kill us all?" Thelma yelped now. "How are we all going to change the world before it blows itself up? Oh, the innocent. Oh, the innocent!" Thelma began shouting. "Oh, the innocent among us poor women."

A staff person, having gotten a drift of the conversation, was now concerned because Thelma was turned on like a flashing red light.

"Oh, sister." Thelma said.

"What happened here?" The staff person, Estelle, asked. "Allegra, are you all right?"

"She's talking to me. Isn't that what you damn people want, to get her talking?"

"Thelma, Allegra is still a new patient."

"Leave this girl to her natural impulses."

"Thelma —"

"No, I'm fine," I said to Estelle. "You don't have to worry. We were just talking."

"Just talking," Thelma repeated.

"Allegra, Dr. Zorn is coming in at ten for a session. You'll be meeting."

"Oh, Dr. Zorn," Thelma groaned. Then laughed as she said, rising, "You and I are going to talk about so many things, too, like Faith Hale." And turning to Estelle, she said, "Oh, honestly. This girl, Allegra, here, is as strong as an axe."

There was a long pause, as if Estelle was now intimidated by this loud, shameless Southern woman who seemed to know important things.

"I'll see you around. Funny thing to say because where the blazes are we all going? What's around?" Thelma said, finally standing. "Ha, ha, ha!" Thelma added: "I have too many damn therapists." She stood tall, dusted off her green chemise, and waving at me said, "Goodbye, sister. Yes, you're a good and valuable sister. *Valuable.* Not everyone in this damn cuckoo's nest knows what 'valuable' means. Or what a sister is in this world. Ha, ha, ha!"

After Thelma had disappeared down the hallway, Estelle pulled up a plain wooden chair and sat close to me. "Allegra, were you bothered by the phone call? Are you feeling calm?"

I couldn't answer because Dr. Zorn suddenly stood in front of me.

"Allegra, how about it?" Dr. Zorn said, "We'll go to the formal gardens."

I stood up. I felt myself swallowing.

"To the gallows, right?" Dr. Zorn said, looking at my drawn face.

The hall felt different whenever Dr. Zorn showed up to talk to me. I stared at the phone down the hallway, now safely in its cradle after hanging up on Faith, and thought for a moment, as I had thought, often: Run. Run as soon as Zorn opens the big front door. Could I go back to Faith? Could I call Faith back and tell her to come and pick me up? That I forgive her at last? Was it still possible that would finally save me? I smelled the morning on Dr. Zorn and, as Dr. Zorn kept moving sideways so I could catch up to her and walk parallel, I swerved myself slightly to the left, allowing myself to walk with Dr. Zorn to the ward's exit doors.

"Did you sleep?" Dr. Zorn asked, putting the key in the lock, and with her thin, small arm holding open the door for me.

"I sleep. Yes, I sleep. That's not the problem," I answered.

And we followed the elegant antique carpeting to the outside of the building, where the rush of winter wind lashed my cheeks, and I felt myself suddenly too cold and wanting to run back to the idle safety of the ward.

"I should have made you take a coat," Dr. Zorn said. "Here, do you want to use mine?" Dr. Zorn pulled her winter coat off her left shoulder before I stopped her, putting my hand out.

"Right," Dr. Zorn said, "You don't expect I would be nice to you. I'm a demon. I think you want to start the struggle again?" Dr. Zorn asked. "I thought this morning we could try talking to one another."

"I don't want to be here. I don't deserve to be here."

"No, you don't."

"I put in another sign-out letter; I expect to be discharged once the three days is up."

"Can I ask you something? Do you feel you got worse after Faith Hale spoke to you?"

"What?"

"I've forbidden her to call again. I feel you were doing well before she called."

I was speechless. We were on the path to the formal gardens for a full session and then suddenly in it, I realized now, the square slabs of stone packed into the ground were the foot guides to the giant garden towards the back of the building. I had gone there before, to the garden which made everything feel like an endless summer. And from there, I could run away. The giant garden had evergreen juniper bushes, giant roses and tulips, and geometric hedges which formed a pattern of bright green rectangles and diamond shapes. The dirt path around the pruned hedge was a deep brown like cocoa. And the statue was an unrecognizable head bust of some 19th-century woman, whom I never found named anywhere, but whom I believed must be the first Mrs. Bloomingdale. The vines bloomed with brightly colored flower cups even in the winter.

Dr. Zorn was making her way to the small, stone bench when suddenly I started running.

If only I knew how I might be able to stop myself from running, I thought. I ran through the evergreen foliage for minutes before I stopped, threw myself down on the ground and began to cry, breathless. The fence separating the hospital from an incline down to a shopping center was in my sight. It was bound to happen, the abscess had to burst, I told myself. Then I closed my eyes and saw a green haze floating. I wanted to hit back at someone, at something, but all I could think about was Faith. I looked around and saw the whole fenced wiring around the incline that led down to the parking lot where the stores lay. It was as if the air were wild with the impossibility of me ever reaching it. I felt Dr. Zorn suddenly beside me. If I slapped Dr. Zorn, I'd make her see all the way to White Plains, I thought. . .if only I could strike this tiny, wiry woman whose prisoner I am.

"OK, that's enough," Dr. Zorn said in a voice sounding as if she was addressing a misbehaving child. "I'm keeping you on closed hall. No more walks outside;

you can't handle it. Now come on, get up, we're going back to the ward."

In my mind, it was a long journey back to the hall. I walked ahead of Dr. Zorn. In the journey, I didn't know what I was afraid of more: the futility of my escape, or never seeing or speaking to Faith again. When I tried to speak, Dr. Zorn said again, "You can't handle it, Allegra." And all that I saw was that I wouldn't escape.

That afternoon, Dr. Zorn told the nurses that I was now on closed hall longer and would not be taken off the hall for any reason. She restricted all phone calls and visits from Faith Hale.

Chapter Nine.

By the twenty-fourth week in this hospital, I was still on close watch because I had found a time the bathroom was empty and tried to hang myself with a blue jean noose. I had breathed in the bathroom's tiled sour-smelling cleanness and pseudo-China floor tiling. It felt soggy in there but clean and clear. By then, I had lost myself and the story I wanted to tell. I had lost the hope of having Faith. She had called again, Faith, but Dr. Zorn wouldn't let me talk to her because she, supposedly, started what Zorn called "the decline." The notion of the imprint was now rebuked by the incarceration I no longer had any control over. In the bathroom, before the hanging, I had whisked up my nightgown and stared into my breasts, my ribcage, slightly protruding, and the very blue swelling veins in my neck. My arms were thin as sticks, but my belly had swelled from the contents of the white machine down the hallway. I wrapped my blue jean legs into a noose, I had simply slipped them out from under my nightgown. They were dirty, these blue jeans, they smelled of the stuffy hall and my desperation. My noose reeked. There I was, positioning myself, trying not to slip off the porcelain rim of the tub, my bare feet unsteady. I placed the blue jean noose around my neck and I wanted to throw myself off the rim into rushing water, but the bathtub was completely dry. A nurse named Judy was suspicious. She told me later she had seen me go into the bathroom "strangely." She'd rushed in almost immediately with her blond hair flip slightly disheveled; she held me until she tugged the noose free off my neck. She got me off the bathtub rim, the blue jean noose falling from her hands after she untied it. I heard her breathing in my ear. "No, you can't," Judy said. I fell to the floor and she quickly sat on top of me. My stomach was to the floor while she crushed my back with her weight. "In here! The bathroom! In here!" Was I out? Because all I remember when I was fully conscious again was the three of them, Judy and two of the younger aides, drawing me up to my feet until one of the aides finally remembered my name and whispered, "No, Allegra, you don't want to — I promise you, you don't want to." "Oh, poor girl," an older aide said, and a siren sounded — an electronic screaming went off from the ceiling somewhere, and soon three more nurses or aides ran rushing into the bathroom.

"But why were you going to do it?" Dr. Zorn asked me moments later in the center lounge. One of the call bells had reached her ears. She had been on the ward and appeared as soon as the nurses shuffled me into the center lounge.

"Let's be alone," was all Dr. Zorn said at first, and as she sat in one of the chairs used for those pointless community meetings, I saw it in her eyes: the reason I wanted so badly to die. Save me, I thought. The same wish I had for Faith. I wanted to be saved. Yearning, though, unleashed a storm in my bowels and I felt the sphincters tighten where my sex was, and a small roll of tears exit from my two eyes, drooling down as from a baby's. Then a pull in my sex, as if a strong man had put me across his lap and was fingering me, orgasms like a stun gun hit me between the legs. Dr. Zorn hadn't touched me except by those two big brown eyes, yet in the wrong areas of love intricately woven into the place my heart ached for just "Mamma's kiss," all internal circuits connected to my sex were accidentally intertwining. I felt myself come, wet, and orgasm. I drew back in horror, in shame so deep I almost stood up and ran from her.

"Oh, my God," I said.

"What is it, Allegra," Dr. Zorn said. I wanted to die more than I ever had, but I did not say that.

"Nothing," I said. "I want to be discharged."

Dr. Zorn put her two slender fingers on her chin. Then, "Stay with me, Allegra, with us, a little while, OK?"

I stared at her in horror.

"Did you have any thought of me when you tied the noose?" She asked suddenly.

"What? Why?" I answered flustered.

"Our closeness?"

"We have no such closeness."

"Can you stay in control, now?"

What was really wrong with me? How much easier it would be if it were romantic love with another woman I was seeking — which made Faith even a greater miracle that abandoned me to the accidental spasms and undifferentiated impulses of my body. I was like a wind-up toy, convulsing, reacting, deficient, undifferentiated.

"The curtain rod wouldn't have held me, it would have torn out of the wall," I said to Dr. Zorn, casting off any such previous reactions to her like a woman trapped in riddles. I closed my eyes, and envisioned the lean, strong boy who had helped me from the river and into the ambulance, and my fears subsided. It was him I wanted here.

"How do you know?" Dr. Zorn asked.

"I want to die," I said finally, alone with the riddle and the absence of cure without Faith. "I want to die."

I don't remember exactly, but when they came, I stood and bolted down toward the nurses' station, and a patient eating yogurt by a table of flowers started laughing as I felt four hands grab ahold of me and thrust me to the carpet. Two nurses grabbed my ankles, and with two other nurses still gripping my ams, I was carried like a piece of meat to its barbeque pit into the sterile white room.

They undid my shirt buttons and said: "Take off your clothes now," just mechanically, as if it were a standard doctor's appointment.

"I'm not taking my clothes off for you to rape me."

"Rape you?" Dr. Zorn was now in the room. "Why would you say rape you, Allegra? You see this?" She held out a plain white starched nightgown that looked more like an apron. "We're going to leave the room. You're going to put it on. We're leaving the room, Allegra. We're leaving." And with that, softly, and cautiously, the nurses and aides followed Dr. Zorn out of the seclusion room, leaving me alone to the white walls.

I am shit, God's waste product, exiled from the angels, I wrote inside my head. I felt something dirty. It will always be true, all living in the self was made impossible by this brutal isolation, like I had been left behind on a planet far away. I carved off a bit of plaster, no bigger than a nickel, and I held it, breathing hard as if I had run miles, and nicked into my left wrist, nicked again and then again until my outside wet in opposition to the internal dissolving. I fell into a madness of cutting.

Chapter Ten.

I spent the two days before Faith came reimagining my old childhood pony shack and a dog I had once named Cassie, who took long strides into the woodsy, undefined land of childhood and whom I loved against my breast as I had wanted to be loved. I closed my eyes and prayed to transform, to another time, to another place. I reached for the walls. What I wanted was my notebook.

I heard the knock and the voices and then I was sure the medication had made me hallucinatory. It was Faith's voice: "Honey, it's Faith," she said, following Dr. Zorn into the white room and shaking. I had never seen Faith scared but she was pallid as the sheet on the quiet room mattress.

"No touching," I quickly heard Dr. Zorn say.

Faith said, "So, here I am. See?"

I stepped away toward the window, scared.

"I'm not coming to hurt you. No more hurting you. Not by you either. They told me." Dr. Zorn nodded meaningfully, but Faith went on. "They said only a few minutes. As I have only a few minutes to tell you I love you, sweetheart. That usually in book time takes a whole story. In your case, sweetheart, many books, I think."

"Mrs. Hale —" Dr. Zorn started.

"I'm leaving, but I'm coming back."

I watched Dr. Zorn put her arm on Faith's shoulder, and slowly they turned their backs on me and that's how slowly a relief came, like a window that had been opened and stayed open just long enough to let the air cool and for the room's wall to look the color of the sky. I didn't think I would ever know what made Dr. Zorn change her mind about me seeing Faith, except I did learn later that Faith had never stopped calling and trying to convince her.

Still, when the door opened two hours later, I was laying on the mattress, cut up by the sliver of plaster on the wall so that both my arms had nicks and were bleeding.

The door opened, and I jumped back.

"Hi, sweetie." It was Faith again, in front of Judy, the nurse.

I looked desperately up and down Faith's boxy body.

"Honey, it's Faith again. It's Faith, Allegra." She patted down her smock dress. "See? Unarmed. I had a long talk with the doctor. They told me you were frightened. Very frightened, that's what they said, I swear. Should I get you a dog or something? This is terrible here."

I heard her laugh, and I took a swallow toward sanity; my tongue reached up to lick my lips. It was a breath and swallow toward endings and how the story eventually ended.

"Mrs. Hale," Judy said. "We need to make this short. You promised."

"Why did you put her in here to begin with?" Faith spun toward Judy, and I watched her untied shoelaces flip-flop over the toes of her sneakers.

"Faith —" I whispered, pointing down to them. If she tripped, it would all be over, I dreaded.

"What honey, it's an honest question."

"Mrs. Hale, the hospital staff thinks the quiet room is the best place for her when she's having such a terrible time. Dr. Zorn agreed to let you see her again. I think that's a lot."

"I'm having a terrible time seeing her here!" Faith said.

"If you'd like to take this up with Dr. Zorn. . ."

Please tie your shoelaces, I thought with the same gravity of hope one might apply to Jesus.

"I'll be back," Faith suddenly said to me. "Don't think I won't talk to Doctor What's-Her-Name again and again."

It was only an hour later that Dory and two other patients stopped by and told me they had seen Faith on the TV once. *The Dick Cavett Show.* The whole hall seemed abuzz with the news that a famous person had come to see me, they said through the quiet room door.

I unpeeled another flake from the quiet room walls, but I did not use it to cut my wrist again. I drew a circle. It etched and in their cemented place some symbol of the imprint and in my own mind that could not translate what had just happened, I tapped on the door until an aide opened it.

"I would like to go to the ladies' room," I told her.

"You —"

"I don't have to explain it to you."

She nodded complacently enough, and I followed her to the large bathroom, where two days prior, I had hung the blue jean noose, and where so many times I believed I couldn't even perform the simple task of the ejection of my bodily fluids. But that time, as if only in a high school girl's room, I let go of the enormous bottling up of the simplest of human practices and I urinated like a celebrity.

Which afternoon did the imprint of Faith return at last to stay? When did I finally say to Faith: "I have to go to court, there's a hearing in two days, and the hospital will say I'm not ready for discharge. That I was be involuntarily committed, for the cutting. The first drowning. The hanging. There would be a judge. I will be involuntarily committed, Faith. Would you come on my behalf to tell them I can be on the outside?"

I wasn't sure which time Faith came to visit I had asked that question and when Faith had answered. "I will."

Court was on a Wednesday afternoon in that January of 1973. Before that, an official had come to me in the center lounge of the hospital a few days before I asked Faith to help me.

"In order to change your status to voluntary, you must go before a hearing," he had explained to me. "You need to understand, if you're an involuntary patient, it will go on your record. You will have been committed. The plan for your commitment would be a total of two years, and you will be in the system."

The cramped courtroom where my hearing was finally held consisted of institutional wood tables, a light tan color. I tried to guess if it was oak or pine that was holding me. Because that was all that was holding me here. The judge sat behind a long table on a platform. There were only three spectators and I didn't know who they were. They were in street clothes, and one of them held a notebook and pen.

Suddenly, the door in the back of the room opened, and I saw Faith coming in. Faith quietly found a seat near to the last row, her lips pale as the light in the room.

Dr. Zorn was with the panel behind the desk next to the judge.

"Case number 309," a woman announced at a desk in front of the platform. I never forgot my number.

The judge presented a litany of statements and questions. "What's going on in the ward?". . ."What is the behavior of the patient?". . ."Is the patient capable of being on voluntary status?" That was all I can and want to remember, except that the judge pointed with his index finger to Faith sitting there. "It is now my understanding that the involuntary status will be reconsidered. Mrs. Hale? You say you will testify on behalf of Ms. Gordon?"

"I will," Faith said to the judge and audience. "I don't think it's right that you keep her committed."

It was Faith who told me to write my story. If not for Faith, I would have been committed, it's true. And I would not have gotten well, I believed. When Faith visited me on the ward, she always brought fruit from Jefferson Market near her apartment. Pears, oval shaped with slashes of dark red for ripeness.

Faith had told the judge at the hearing I was a real writer and, with help, would survive all of this. And that she would oversee all my writing. She had seen some already and called it "exquisite." And she also brought in the outside world, dressed in her plain jean skirts, and Keds sneakers. Her hair, mostly unruly, except for the part that was pulled together and set into a bun on the top of her head which was careful, conscientiously made, precise as her written sentences. Her face — so serious, I thought, with eyes widened and alerted by the ward's closed spaces, its windowless imprisonment. She smelled like special soap, I didn't know which brand, but it was obvious Faith bathed and prepared for these visits like a young girl going to a serious place. Her sentences were short and clipped, answering the nurses in formal ways: "Yes, hello. My name is Faith Hale." "I'm fine, thank you." And always, "Is she here?" I always was there, and we took over the center lounge with my notebook and her eyes. Her squared body was tensed and she always pushed out her lower lip, as if trying not to say anything, but on guard in case she must.

I would go into the dining room on the ward every night at eight to pound out my scenes on an Olivetti typewriter Faith bought for me. Faith had volunteered at the hearing to help me write and to publish — it was what saved me from being involuntarily committed for years. Of my writing, Faith had not only told the judge it was "exquisite," but also that it was "coherent and professsional."

I wrote about the mental hospital and the people in it. And about why I ended up there. And if such a place like the locked ward for women should even exist in a fair world. The mental hospital was wrong, as Faith had said during the hearing. Now I could write with some privacy, except I had to keep the dining room door slightly opened, and some nights it had to stay fully open.

"It's like this," I wrote a few weeks after Faith came from the hearing to the hospital to visit, "the imprint: I imagine it as a magical oval circle, red as blood, as if the giver had opened inside me, like a pod. It is like a motor that is running that reaches right through me under my skin and I awaken, enlivened, and I survive. I stole your imprint, Faith. I am a thief of love, Faith."

There was an iridescence to everything those weeks after Faith began to visit, as if instead of the drab and sorrowful world I knew, things were lighted and warmed. I no longer needed the suicide watchers. The hospital world was dissolving as the "imprint" on Faith took hold, the dark states less frequent. It was decided I would remain a voluntary patient, then an outpatient. I stayed for a few more weeks, writing with Faith visiting.

There were bare tables, chairs up on them, and the sterile smells of floor scrubs and the dishwasher. Every night I would write, under the blaze of the fluorescent light on the ceiling and the sight of an aide peeking through the curtain on the top of the door.

I had, since Faith came to claim me, at last stepped into my dream, I sometimes felt. When I go to my writing desk even now, years later, Faith is there. It is a spell. I told Faith when I went to the patient library to look up ancient forms of sorcery, I had found "Maria, the alchemist of ancient Babylon in the second century" who, like Faith, performed feats of transformation by stirring raw mercury into a soup she fed women stricken with hysteria.

I also told Faith about Ferdinand Magellan, who I learned had discovered for himself that planet Venus was covered with opaque clouds made of sulfuric acids, showing evidence of "extreme volcanism," which, like my mental illness, was held in the grip of the merciless Milky Way.

"History is good," Faith had said.

I don't know if she believed me about the imprint, which I finally spouted out to her once I was close to discharge in late March.

"I have an imprint inside of you, do you believe me?" I asked, then I showed her what I had written about it.

All she said was "women need women," and added: "Whatever you call it, sweetie."

I think Faith believed me.

Chapter Eleven.

New York, August, 1988.

I put my hand out now to turn on the shower water and it ran at me, warm as toast. Quickly, I reached for the lever that regulated the temperature and switched it toward "cold." Water flowed under my underpants, and it aroused me. Too much thinking, I thought. The day was approaching, and I was to meet my brother, Julian, at the docks to talk about Sofia. I had planned to leave as soon as possible after for Faith's. I would go see Faith in Vermont that afternoon, but all I wanted to do at the moment was go back to sleep, give in to the fatigue that seemed to be replacing my excitement about the trip to Faith's. My tiredness came as a cloud covered up direct sunlight, slowly, gloomily, restricting light and warmth.

Finally, after a few minutes, I got myself out of the shower, threw a blue towel around my waist, and pushed down the wet panties. I crept back into the bedroom where Michael was still not there, went to my underwear drawer, and put on a fresh pair. Then I went into the kitchen and filled the coffee machine with water. There would be time to sort out my thoughts. Watching the coffee machine, I sat down at the kitchen table. There was a box of rusks in the cabinet, but they would make me think of Faith and the first time I met her in her office, so many years ago. I poured some black coffee out of a mug in the bathtub. It was warm as a summer wind.

I walked into the living room where I had been writing the previous night.

My notebook was open on the small table near the curtains of the living room, and pages had scattered under the table in the rush to get the packing done for today's trip to Vermont later that day.

I looked down at the notepad where, beneath a stain of tuna fish salad, I had scribbled:

> Weep no more, woeful shepherds,
> weep no more,
>
> For Lycidas, your sorrow, is not dead.
> Sunk though she be beneath the
> watery floor.
> (John Milton, "Lycidas")
>
> I am the girl who can enjoy
> invisibility.
> (James Joyce, Ulysses)

That's what I had wanted to tell Faith in the dream that early morning; I had changed a word in Ulysses from "boy" to "girl" and the "he" to "she" in Milton's line. And they had affected a chapter in my new novel. Who else but Faith would care to know, or understand why?

The doctors didn't want me committed ever again since Faith came and testified on my behalf. I married Michael, a psychiatric resident at Payne Whitney in 1977. I was "in love" as he was fascinated by my darkness, a strict disciplinarian kind of male with a taciturn demeanor, Lutheran background, and an inability to let go as much as I was wildly too able to let go.

The street noise, the clamor of refugees from mental institutions and halfway houses who crowded the city's public quarters, filled the city. These quarters had become the new Ellis Island for immigrants coming from the institutions — parks and spaces near the shelters, filled with furnitured tarps, cardboard box beds, and plastic bedding with filthy blankets, scattered clothes and shoes, and sometimes paperback books on philosophy or any other subject, fiction or nonfiction, begged for or bought from the street peddlers selling books outside on tables for fifty cents or less. The sewer life felt like paradise for the people who had freedom there, who had nothing, but escaped those who accused them of being nothing, silencing outside judgment as I had silenced Sofia and others.

The urine-stinking wastelands were under brick buildings and tarps to protect the shelters they made on the street. The streets brimming over with anonymous faces and bodies, deinstitutionalized, intimate colonies, were springing up everywhere.

I remembered where I went for one of my walks earlier that week. The East River was spitting its debris on its banks littered with soda and beer cans, children's rubber balls, department store trinkets, wrappers, plastic jewelry, and little emblematic trinkets and amulets hung inside taxicabs. Once I saw a condom floating toward me as I waded in the waters below First Street and beyond Avenue A.

I thought then, as I had in the mental hospital, that only the homeless and "mentally ill" were beacons of light and wisdom, and I had started spending more of my time on the city streets with the homeless, and with my notebooks writing about them. I wondered if all the immigrant cab drivers threw their good luck amulets and beads out into the dirty city streets once they realized the amulets didn't work. I had read in the papers this summer the city had begun dredging the East River, running water tests, draining and oxidizing the waste. Parts of the river were clear; I saw fishermen by the lower streets, near where the river reached toward the Avenue C tenements.

What would have happened to me if Faith hadn't been there, I asked myself, shuddering. My book about the people of the long-term hospital I wrote with Faith eight years ago was published by a small press Faith found for me. The book received good notice and reviews, enough for me to keep writing. I went to the notebook and looked at the new pages. How was I to remember everything? I was writing about Faith and the hospital.

"Is Faith there?" I called later that morning. I had spent the rest of the morning sifting through my old notebooks and perusing the sheets of a new novel. My Manhattan apartment smelled like old bed sheets in the afternoons. I wondered if Faith's sickroom in Vermont was as mercilessly damp and hot. The humidity in the air was enough to extinguish someone, I thought.

Now it was Faith who was sick.

"Who is this?" asked the person on the other end of the telephone. I had never been asked that when I called Faith's house. I clasped my elbow, balancing the phone receiver under my neck, on my shoulder.

"Allegra," I said. "It's Allegra Gordon."

"Hi, Allegra." I recognized the voice of Faith's graduate student, Laura. Faith's "personal assistant" was what Laura called herself, I remembered. We had met briefly a few weeks ago at Faith's apartment in New York the afternoon *Time* magazine did an interview with Faith. It was just after Faith won some huge literary prize, but I couldn't remember which one.

"Faith can't come to the phone right now," Laura said, "I don't think Faith will be able to come to the phone tonight, either. Her cancer has been getting more difficult." Laura's voice was hesitating, as if she didn't quite remember who I was.

"You see, I've just about finished packing," I said, "I guess Faith may not have mentioned to you that we talked a few days ago, I'm taking the Peter Pan bus up to her later this afternoon. I should be there late tonight. Would Faith like me to bring her something from the city? Could you ask her please?"

"Oh, no, no. You can't come up."

"I promised Faith I would be visiting her."

"Yeah, well," she started. "Faith's too sick with the cancer. Okay, I need to get back to her." Abruptly, Laura hung up.

The assistant's echo seemed to hang in the air like a warden's key locking up her prisoner for the night. Something else, too, was weaving through the air, like a warning, or a whisper of approaching flames. A foreboding. I felt bankrupt. I sat down on the couch to stop the dizzying emptiness, the blow — what to call it?

I looked toward the living room door, remembering the plain wooden file cabinet where I had stored those notebooks from years ago.

Faith and I and the times we had sat together in that center lounge of broken people in 1973, eating peanut butter and saltines. I wondered more than a few times as I advanced, after that day, later taking my seat again and again at the window to write for Faith in her city apartment, staring often at the linden trees on her block, and hearing their leaves as spirits in my head, if her imprint had been a miracle for me. The phone was always ringing in her apartment: strangers arrived with strange and sometimes scary stories of heartbreak that Faith famously hugged and kissed away with her outsized personality.

What was true? The times we huddled in her tiny bedroom when her daughter and husband were in Vermont. That it felt good; she had set me up with a writing desk in her living room after my release, and we both were writing, she her poetry in the kitchen.

Faith and I shopped on Fourteenth Street, where there were tiny stores overfilled with cheap dresses and shirts, that made us feel like we were at a carnival.

"I'll buy it for you," Faith once said. "Look — only three dollars!"

"Yes?" said the owner of the street store. "Can I help you?"

"No, you can't," Faith said roughly, as if meaning he couldn't cure either of us. "But you can let me buy this dress for my friend."

Slowly, when we got back to her apartment after shopping, I had pulled down the incessant "mental patient" blue jeans, and it was as if there was a smell let loose from my body into the room, a smell like the linden tree below her window.

By the middle of March that year, I had been there, in Faith's West Village apartment several times. Below the living room window was that linden tree and a nest of tulips. Faith periodically went down to the street to water them and appreciate them. Her apartment was toppling over with letters, people's manuscripts, invitations; so even the lived-in parts looked like a messy office.

The train station in Bronxville, and that cab ride from Grand Central which took me to Faith's, were luxurious to me after the hospital and all that immobility, the paralysis, and the illness had wrought in me.

The last time I saw Faith was a few weeks ago, in the Great Hall at Cooper Union. I sat in my usual front row seat with Faith, remembering how Faith used to grab my hand in wild, uninhibited affection and tell me to sit beside her. The Great Hall contained huge white columns and a history swelling with meaning and overwhelming importance — Abraham Lincoln's debates, the Union Maids, and early feminist suffragettes of the 1920s — as if they were framing me in the same pictures, the line-up of the famous. Walt Whitman's famous poem, "Song of the Open Road," was inscribed into the chestnut frame of his portrait: "You light that wraps me and all things in delicate equable showers! You paths worn in the irregular hollows by the roadsides! I believe you are latent with unseen existences, you are so dear to me."

I had felt that light, I thought, and it was the way I might have heard about it in some mystic's novel. Sitting so close to Faith just that way, through some symbiotic luminescence, I shone too. The input of Faith's light into me gave me light.

But this last time at Cooper Union, Faith's touch had been so fragile, Faith's hand slipping back onto an empty seat on the other side of me as if she didn't realize I had sat down. Faith, reduced by cancer that summer, looked so vulnerable, stripped. Her jokes came less frequently, and Faith's fiercely affectionate hugs, which had once made me feel like a sweet pleasure was all around us — protecting and embalming me against intruders — now was only the feel of Faith's weakened, skinny arms, brittle and unsteady. Faith's face was struck by the cancer, too, unnaturally white and sinuous. Her back stooped, almost spineless, or as if what spine she had left was string. Then, to make it all worse, Faith wore a wig — a gray and blonde wig, too big for her skull she had picked out haphazardly with her daughter, Deborah — for a reason I didn't understand.

"Deborah and I went out and picked out a few wigs," Faith had said. "I liked this one, at least or because it isn't dopey." Faith left for Vermont that next day, I called her in the morning, and she answered in her kitchen chewing a piece of bread, as she always did when talking. She hadn't been back in Manhattan since then.

Too much thinking, I thought in the living room. It was already early afternoon, and I was to meet Julian at the docks soon. My trip to Vermont was thwarted. Laura, the assistant, had trapped me, blocked my escape to Faith's house. I would have to call Michael, too — later after he'd come back to New York and had gone to his office and tell him I was going to Vermont. But all I really wanted was to put my body down on the floor, close my eyes, give in to the overwhelming fatigue that seemed to be replacing my excitement about the trip to Faith's. The tiredness came as a cloud covers up direct sunlight, slowly, gloomily, restricting light and warmth.

My notebook was open, and pages had scattered under the bed in the rush to get the packing done in time for today's trip to Vermont.

Looking down at the notepad where, beneath a stain of tuna fish salad, I had scribbled yesterday, I read:

Weep no more, woeful shepherds, weep
no more,

For Lycidas, your sorrow, is not dead.
Sunk though she be beneath the
  watery floor.
(John Milton, "Lycidas")

> I am the girl who can enjoy
> invisibility.
> (James Joyce, <u>Ulysses</u>)

That's what I had wanted to tell Faith in the dream this morning; I had changed a word in Ulysses from "boy" to "girl". And it had affected a chapter in my new novel, that ineffable confusion I was never able to express. Who else but Faith would care to know, or understand why.

We would talk soon, and the heat would soon infiltrate the outside city air. The city was exhausting in August, and I had to meet my brother at five by the docks to talk about Sofia, who was failing, overrun with age.

"What do you think, that I'm scared, Allegra?" Faith had said to me in a recent phone conversation, before that assistant had taken charge of her. "I'm scared for the people I'm leaving for good, for instance, close friends and my family. I'm scared also for Don. Can Don be alone? I wonder how he will go on. I'm not scared for you, and I'm not scared of it, darling, you can say the words you know, out loud. I mean, you can say 'death' in front of me."

At the beginning of the summer, Faith had been abandoned on an East Village Street, her back stooped, that funny knitted hat perched on the ill-fitting wig she used to cover up her balding head. She had refused to use a cane when the cancer took the balance straight out of that hefty, no-nonsense strut. A strut that once demonstrated the confidence of all caring towards the constantly threatened planet, and an abstract "everybody." It was as if her strong walk once was meant to broadcast that she had more than enough backbone to take on the world. But a young poetess Faith had supported abandoned Faith on the street that day. The poetess walked too fast for Faith's stricken legs to keep up and turned a corner on Hester Street, and simply left Faith stranded. If not for me, refusing to race ahead, if not for me, who for several months had watched over Faith, Faith might have fallen. The chemo had started; she was weak in all her bones.

"Faith," I had whispered. "Here, I've got you, Faith," my arm went around Faith's emaciated back. "Screw her, Faith," I had said.

"No, no," Faith said, becoming fierce, "she's a very good poet! She's had such a hard life, why should she trust anyone, including me?" Faith could never condemn anyone.

Faith called me sometimes just to tell her old stories about West Village — The Jefferson Market, the prostitutes and famous political activists jailed together in the Women's House of Detention.

I should call Faith now, I thought. Maybe the assistant was off duty by now. I would soon have to leave for my meeting with Julian.

All that previous week, the telephone calls had been pounding in on me, making me feel gifted with the wild importance of being Faith's messenger — from Faith's mentees, protégés, "sisters and daughters in prose" (as someone had remarked in *O, The Oprah Magazine*), to emails from the President of the National Organization for Women, an association of women tabulating statistics on how many women novelists got full reviews in *The New York Times*, and if their already bestselling books were getting as much attention as their male counterparts, and if not, could women's literature survive? Would I consent to an interview about what Faith Hale, the original feminist, would say about this? Then, there was the filmmaker who wanted to do a documentary on Faith but couldn't get to Faith's remote farmhouse in Vermont and had repeatedly called me. The filmmaker had plaintively asked me: "But how can I get there? I don't know how to get all this film equipment there either, and anyway, do you know if Faith would want to be filmed in her present state? She wears a wig now, for heaven's sake. Please, could you tell Faith I'm a good person, I can be trusted? It's a feminist film. What if you call Faith and read her my questions, and you write the answers down and then tell me her answers?" Then there was the competing filmmaker with the Guggenheim grant and then the Code Pink delegates who phoned yesterday. Could Code Pink please know the exact words of the quote Faith made about "resistance" and talking "truth to power?" They needed to quote Faith on the tee-shirts they were making for the campaign against the Israeli occupation in Gaza. A delegation from Code Pink was going on a boat (or did they say a ship?) to Egypt. Once they reached Egypt, they would meet with the leader of the Islamist group, Hamas.

When did I start feeling like a doorway people just walked through on their way to Faith? The phone would ring again; it would be more of Faith's friends, a rain of voices pouring on me.

"Please tell her I love her."

"Darling, do you have any more news about Faith?"

"I hope I'm not bothering you, but would you happen to have Faith's number in Vermont?"

"What do you think? Should I call her? Can you ask her if it's all right for me to call her? When can you get back to me on this?" When had all this begun?

Perhaps the very last line I would have to cherish in the intimate privilege of being close to Faith Hale was, "Put the water on, would you, toots?" which had made me happy, like the warm odors of cheese and creamed herrings left out on Faith's kitchen table; fresh loaves of rye and raisin bread on a cutting board beside a serrated knife to slice them; and strong, fresh coffee brewing on Faith's stove. Faith was always interrupted by what felt like a stream of never-ending phone calls. I always preferred the author's photo of Faith in a gingham dress, when her hair was long and unruly. The photo peeked out from a shelf in my living room, over my writing desk. An afghan was over Faith's lap in the photo. I saw pictures of Faith's parents' Russian city, Odessa, on top of Faith's chest of drawers in her office in an article; there were black and white photos showing the shabby lettering on the Odessa signboards, the stones of the houses, and women with tall hairdos standing gazing into forests. It was, too, the city of my father's parents, though I had not known that for a long time until I made the connection to Faith's family photos. I had let myself fantasize that Faith was a Russian woman in Odessa, the city facing the Black Sea; sunning in a vast field of sand at the seaport. Light Russian winter, and all around, hawks, predatory blackbirds. The snow falling harder, mercilessly, but, as if in a dank basement, the smell of musty, warm sweat, because I was under Faith's skirt in the fantasy. The snow could fall, the howls of wind and swooping birds could sound, but I would only hear my own voice breathing. The places where Faith's sex might have been were terrifying to encounter for me. But in the long voyage down, hugging Faith's knees, I told myself this was a different kind of love; this was not that kind of love, though there was excitement and trembling in my body, as I felt filled with Faith. Faith's high breasts were like two small, tight sacks stuffed with feathers. And in this tent of Mother, I remained safe.

It was mysterious to me why the older famous writer liked to tell me the stories of the waiting room at the cancer clinic, about the Russian patient who was drawing a mural on the walls. What did he draw, I had wondered? What were his images? Were they the same as the photos on Faith's wall in her West Tenth Street apartment — the Russian forests and countrysides? "You should see this mural that he paints. What a painter! He does it to tell his story." Faith had said. "Isn't that so interesting?" Faith added, "But you know all about trying to tell your story, don't you, toots?" Then she paused. "I remember those first stories when you looked at the people around you, you know, those people in the mental hospital, their community, which was yours, too."

Now Faith's own death approached like an inexorable limping animal that I could not caress and embrace. I feared the "imprint" would dissolve if Faith were no longer around to conjure it. Even with Michael in my life.

It wasn't always like this. There was a time when people refused to believe that Faith had anything to do with me. After I finished my first book, I had sent a note to *O, The Oprah Magazine*, asking if they would look at my first book and review it. It had been published by a small press Faith funded called Bedford Hill Press, and Faith Hale was the editor and publisher of my work. Eventually, she wrote a message to the editor-in-chief at that magazine.

The editor responded vigilantly to my note: "Faith Hale? Really? I don't think so. It sounds like you're just using her name. Was this really a message from Faith Hale? I think your ploy of using that on your subject line to get our attention is disrespectful and off-putting." The editor didn't say: "You should be ashamed," but that's what I felt. I was angry enough to write the editor back in fury and demand an apology from her, showing her a number of press releases and reviews. "Please accept our apologies for the misunderstanding," the editor wrote. "We are always extremely cautious when people invoke the names of well-known personalities — as you can imagine, we are highly protective of their name and feel the same way about all our friends, including Ms. Hale. Your note did not refer to Bedford Hill Press until the very end, and so it was not immediately clear that you are in fact published by Faith Hale's press." I found out later from Faith that she had no idea who this editor was — and was hardly a "friend" of hers. "Nope, never heard of her," Faith said sympathetically to me.

Still, I had been ashamed of what I had done, contacting that magazine, and I was also ashamed after being dismissed by Laura that morning, because needing Faith was unbearable again, the loss threatening the whole room. It was as if all the furniture in the room was going to be suddenly towed away, leaving me alone inside a barren, unlivable space. I needed to make that call to Faith, but I dreaded I would reach the assistant Laura, again, instead.

I went back to the bedroom where Michael would have been still sleeping soundly on his side if he were here. His massive body would leave me ample room as was always true; more than enough room. I thought again of how I had allowed myself a breathless, unabashed, full love for Michael these years; he was where all love was during and after the psychiatric hospital, an intimacy, shining hotly, unmatched by anything outside us.

After shutting my eyes the previous night and trying to sleep, I had instead slipped off the edge of the mattress into a small crevice under the bookshelves. The crevice was where we stored the sundry things the closets had no room for. I had landed on the bag filled with Michael's snorkeling equipment and a few loose blankets and, crossing my arms across my chest, I stayed there, sandwiched between the built-in bookshelves and the ridged bottom of the bed, smelling the old stowed-away rugs, rolled up posters, knick-knacks and trinkets, the sweet dust from the hundred books or more Michael and I had in the bookshelves — paperbacks dating back to college days. Michael's medical journals and case notes from his residency in psychiatry, albums of the times we had gotten away and taken cheap trips to Europe, Panama, and the Middle East. But sometimes I believed that it was Michael's huge body taking up all my space, bullying me into a corner as if I were an unwanted load of nothing; I was haunted often by irrational fears of his dominance. Where Faith was sure annihilation would come from the manmade world in nuclear explosions, I lay in terror of my own imploding hopelessness and rage against the powerlessness and submission I felt while loving Michael or any man or anyone. It was also because of Faith long ago at the hospital that I could have let him in at all.

Now, instead of staying in the bedroom, I went into the cluttered living room to try to nap. I pulled out one of Michael's old medical school textbooks for a pillow, hoping I could read myself into a nap, if necessary. I tried to fall asleep but, too charged, I lifted the book and stared through its contents. Some of its pages had showed a woman's breast x-rayed into colorful arteries and secret sacs. "What is the breast?" I read:

> The breast generally refers to the front of the chest and medically specifically to the mammary gland. The word 'mammary' comes from 'mamma, the Greek and Latin word for the breast, which derives from the cry 'mama' uttered by infants and young children.

How are human breasts different
from those of other primates?
What are other internal features of
the breast?
There are no muscles in the breasts.

I will go to visit Faith, I told myself now. I needed
to see Faith.

Filled with resolve, I jumped up and went to my
TUMI bag in the bedroom. I needed to feel strong to
face the "personal assistant." No one had the right to
take Faith away from me. I opened my desk drawer and
pulled out the Peter Pan schedule. A bus ran at 8 pm to
Burlington.

I had plenty of time. If I met Julian late this afternoon, I could make it back in time to catch the Burlington bus. It seemed like the perfect plan. Get the bus
ticket. See Julian by the East River docks. I rehearsed my
lines silently: "Yeah, well, Julian, Mami was always like
that, doesn't ever want to rely on anyone or feel helpless.
Yeah, I know, I know we have to put her somewhere; she
can't keep up the maintenance on the house. I get it."

I felt hungry thinking about going up to Faith's. I
should make myself a sandwich; there would be no food
on the Peter Pan bus. I'd get a room in Burlington, no
fuss. All I really needed was two pairs of jeans and a few
shirts; did I overpack? What can you wear in August in
Vermont? It was cooler in Vermont, I was sure — all
those rivers and hills Faith described, the forests, the
raccoons, and deer. A warm feeling came back.

I started to pack my smaller toiletry bag with sham-
poo and sundries into the TUMI bag, with a steady
thrust of purpose and resolve now. When I was finished
packing my toiletry bag, I went into the kitchen. I bent,
opened the kitchen cabinet under the sink, pulled out

the Brillo pads, and ran the hot water over last night's dirty dishes. I applied myself willingly, energetically, to cleaning the bathroom, collecting myself, then taking a decent shower this time.

In my shower, the water was pleasantly lukewarm, and I felt lightened, relieved. All that seemed left to do was to plan some Lean Cuisine frozen dinner in the freezer for Michael's dinner tonight and make his next-day sandwich lunch. But I could do that after I met with Julian for the talk about my mother and what to do with her now that, like Faith, she was in old age. And I would arrive in Burlington late at night, and the stars would be out, I told myself.

It was an hour later when the phone rang.

"Allegra?" It was Don, Faith's husband, his warm, but tough New England voice.

"Don. . ."

"Look here now," he said. "I wanted to tell you — Laura told me you called here earlier."

My heart seemed to bite me, was he, too, going to forbid my trip?

"See, well, Allegra, Faith died an hour ago. I wanted to let you know. Yep, we lost her."

I fell into the couch, my back slapping against its backboard. Then I sat up fast, dizzyingly. "Oh, Don. . ."

"She was delusional, in the bed, I mean — she really was out of it, mumbling and such. What the hell was she trying to say?" I heard him breathing deeply, wet, saddened breaths in silence, and then I knew I had to let him go.

"Don, if you need anything —"

"Yeah, yeah," he said.

"I'm — I loved her," I finally said.

"And she you," Don said, before I could get another word out, "And she loved you."

Chapter Twelve.

Days later, a line of people wound down a West Village street toward the opening in the iron gates of the communal garden at Twelfth Street and Sixth Avenue. It would have been right to have all the shops closed in tribute to Faith, I thought — the shopkeepers at the hair studio, the bakery and drugstore personnel perhaps taking a moment to notice that the short, grey-haired woman who wrote about them and their neighborhood wasn't around anymore. But, my head cleared and I soon saw it was a business day as usual, an ordinary late September Wednesday, with customers in the nearby shops. Then, I was thinking, this is the tribute Faith would have wanted, to be part of the ordinary movements of ordinary people.

Days had passed since Faith's death. I hadn't grieved, I hadn't been able to write. This was the fifth tribute I would attend. The funeral had been in Vermont, and I hadn't gone because I wasn't on whatever list. I felt more fragile than I had in years, even when I was invited to gatherings to talk about Faith, or to read Faith's work to audiences. I wasn't sure why. It was as if everybody was too loud and authoritative about Faith. Because my love for Faith was stronger than my terrible self-doubts, and her belief in me and my writing kept me alive, I could not let this happen — the endless tributes, articles and interviews about Faith going on without my voice. I owed Faith that much. The imprint was still alive inside.

The papers had been kind to the memory of Faith Hale. "Faith Hale, a much beloved and admired writer and political activist whose short stories were celebrated for their pitch-perfect dialogue, rich language, and exploring the everyday struggles of ordinary women, died on Wednesday at her home near Burlington, Vermont. She was eighty-four. 'I'm not interested in the famous and wealthy,' Faith Hale once said, 'I want to portray the lives of ordinary people and their opened-ended fates.' Ms. Hale was among the earliest American women writers to write directly about the lives of women in all their dailiness, their mix of sexual appetites, lusts, family obligations, insecurities, and their uncharted inner lives. . ."

There were exceptions. In *The New York Review of Books*, a well-known writer intimated that Faith Hale had an affair with Donald Barthelme, which I knew never happened. Many of Faith's stories had been about women and men crushed by infidelity. A political blog had misrepresented Faith as in favor of the extremist group Hamas in Gaza, also untrue. The cartoon storyboard was usually the same, too. Faith, stirring the crowd into a trancelike state against the political system and toward moral corruption in the country, and doing so much as a shaman would, but clothed in an ordinary woman's house dress or skirt. A writer's organization offered a solemn, grandiose photograph of Faith Hale uncharacteristically posing in a photo much as a political leader might — presidential, smile-less, and somber — above a quote of her saying — "Let us go forth with fear and courage and rage to save the world." A blog declared its mission as being to "celebrate this amazing woman (Faith Hale) and record nonviolent actions around the world to further her vision of resistance to the empires of war and exploitation." Quotes from Faith Hale were used on political banners and tee-shirts, regardless of the cause. Various political organizations commemorated Faith Hale's anti-war ideology to support their positions, though it was often doubtful that Faith's views were compatible. People told personal stories, often exaggerating their intimacy with Faith Hale. One recounted sitting on her lap like a child and weeping while she mothered her into well-being.

The icon, Faith Hale, was growing to be thought of as a grand, Gandhi-like heroine, a political radical making solemn leadership speeches to bands and stadiums full of politically aroused and feverish followers.

Faith Hale as a cultural phenomenon, an icon, was created.

I took out the scotch I had packed in my handbag in anticipation of how I might feel at this tribute, my usual expensive single malt I poured into an empty vitamin bottle these days to disguise as a health drink. My mind swirled as the pleasant, familiar sensations of scotch cruised through me.

My thoughts returned to the empty week of daily mind-numbing phone calls. And to my own piece for *The Washington Post* — "My friends and I used to call Faith Hale's West Village apartment 'headquarters' because she was the mother of our needy female selves. And we all needed her maternity so much. I first met her decades ago when I was an insecure sophomore at Abigail Stone College. . ."

How could I have written something so girlish and effusive? It embarrassed me afterward. I had twice thought of calling the *Post* to pull the story, but hadn't gone through with it.

Scattered memories about the years with Faith were crowding my mind while waiting on the line at the tribute. I couldn't help it. I started thinking of the times I had felt, seen, and heard. What if soon, the imprint would dissolve? Would it be that I would have to go back to the hospital?

"We have a guest on our show," Dick Cavett had announced a day Faith appeared on *The Dick Cavett Show* again a second time. "She has found herself in a very special situation. She is awaiting trial after being arrested on the White House lawn with other protestors. . .." I had been in the audience that day. I had wandered backstage to try to help Faith put her hair up with a plastic barrette and pull down her plain housedress. It was the first time I saw Faith wear heels, bright red, low heels, and Faith walked out onto the stage with the same forward thrust to her pelvis, thick short legs supporting her like bedposts.

Now, in the garden tribute, I gazed up at the high tower of Jefferson Library. It reassured me that something real and substantial of the many walks and conversations with Faith through this neighborhood might endure.

"The sky — this vault of hope and desire, love and sadness. . .at least they can't divide the sky." I suddenly remembered Christa Wolf's words one morning at Faith's apartment. Faith had sheltered both the exiled Christa Wolf, an internationally famous East German writer, and me. The depressed figure of Christa Wolf, who was said to have been an informant to the East German Stasi, was nestled in the bed sheets in Faith's room, a dark mass of body, need, and guilt. She had contracted food poisoning from something she had picked up from a street vendor. "Shush, OK, Cookie," Faith had said to me, greeting me at the door that morning. She had come to the door holding a pillow from the living room couch. "We have a visitor who is not very happy. It's Christa Wolf; you went to her reading, do you remember? She is in great distress. And she's in despair so dense it paralyzed her — the way you were." I had nodded. Then I had walked into Faith's kitchen. I imagined the long night Faith and Christa Wolf had together. I wondered if Faith had talked to her about bagels and how "the Jefferson Market is expanding" in between conversations about how the Berlin Wall fell and how Wolf didn't remember informing on other writers to the Stasi now that communism was over, that "it was all a blank to her." The soft, depressed, and tender Christa Wolf emerging from Faith's bedroom stayed in my mind, as well as Christa eating Faith's favorite rye bread from the West Village bakery, and her cheeses from Murray's later that day. I ate the same bread and cheese as the famous German writer that day in 1986.

Love is how Faith did it, I thought — how, through her full-bodied warmth, she offered a kind of salvation to those who visited her, as I had done often, visiting her depressed again.

All that tea and Jefferson Market rye bread, I thought, all those tangerines. How could I ever explain that small apartment full of figures with rough edges, intense, recognizable faces? I could not even remember half their names.

I took another gulp from my bottle now. The scotch wouldn't tranquilize me. I put it back in my purse.

The line to the outdoor tribute was advancing, and I walked slowly with it, following the woman in front of me. The iron gates were wide open, and I finally entered the garden with the others.

I had not been invited to read at any of the important tributes, which were filled only with famous young writers who barely knew Faith. At Cooper Union before PEN America's major tribute to Faith Hale, I sat in the same hall I used to sit with Faith holding my hand, but this time I was amid a crowd of Faith's old friends and was hustled into a glass-topped section of the lobby before the tribute performance started inside the auditorium.

When I got inside the Cooper Union auditorium after waiting inside the glass-topped cubicle, I was guided to separated seats on the right side of the big room. I was standing, sucking in my breath and anger, as I perused the guest speakers, most of whom Faith barely knew but who were high-profile authors, seated in another separated section in front of the seat I was assigned.

A woman of a couple tapped me on the shoulder arching her eyebrow. "Can we get a program please?"

The couple that thought I was the usher sat behind me two rows, and I could hate, I had thought, I could hate more than I ever, ever had hated. I had turned myself around quickly.

I shook my head of the memory, too bitter.

Being in the garden was a relief. It was filled with manufactured bubbling brooks and patches of magnolia flowers — all different species: saucer magnolias, star magnolias, plain yellow, and vibrant magnolias. Scattered amid the crab apple and dogwood trees, grey wooden benches were along the pathway. Standing at a distance from the collected group on the grass, I suddenly felt some of the others in the garden were staring at me. I was sure I could not make myself vanish.

In the middle of the garden, standing among the orchids, Japanese roses, and bushes of all varieties, was the filmmaker I remembered from phone calls and different events. Esther Kaplan was her name. The filmmaker stood perched to record the images on the signs members of the crowd held. "Faith presente" was written on several signs. I recognized the Spanish from old postcards from Argentina in

Sofia's drawers. They were Latin Catholic sayings about the immortality of the soul, and a few of these hand-scrawled signs were held up into the mercifully warm and dry midmorning. They were thrust against and alongside political signs that said: "This is what a feminist looks like" and several generic anti-violence signs. Most of the attendees were trouser-bearing, strong-faced women.

I spotted a stray street person wandering in from the Perry Street entrance with leaves stuck to her sooty hair, a scarecrow image as thin as the unwanted wild plants growing in between the beds of magnolias and Japanese roses. This one bewildered street person, a stranger whose stink, I thought, must be excruciating to those in Faith's following and who forced my mind to go backward in time remembering the many times I went to Faith's apartment as the other me, the mental patient. What was plaguing me since Faith's death was that I, the most unlikely candidate to take up the responsibility of continuing Faith Hale's legacy somehow — the girl who had reveled in self-ruminations, and bouts of self-hate, in suicide and mental hospitals, of playing the village idiot in order to remain a child guided or teased or softly beaten — would somehow have to, at last, rise to the urgency of preserving and protecting Faith Hale's afterlife and a crucial part of her legacy.

The trees behind me seemed to weigh on me, as if they were bending in the breezeless air, lying heavy and non-retractable on my back. I looked around at the assembled crowd. They were all strangers to me, except for the few older Abigail Stone students, whom I had barely communicated with through the years. Most of them still looked like college students, just aged versions with graying, unstylish, mussed hair, wearing the same jeans and tee-shirts they did in college, or cheap summer floral-printed shifts, like Faith wore, bought at the street shops on Fourteenth Street.

"Here I am on the family front porch. . ." Someone was reading a Faith Hale poem now, jolting me with the drone of their reciting voice:

> In the garden, rocking in a rocking chair, large thighs apart under a big skirt. . .
>
> A pleasant summer sweat. . .

I again perused the assembly as he quoted. Looking at the gardener's hut and the small green house, I remembered Faith telling me about the Women's House of Detention, which once stood where this garden was now. "There were a lot of prostitutes locked up there, it's true," Faith had told me, "but, also there were all these 'big shots' like Ethel Rosenberg, Angela Davis, Evelyn Nesbit, and What's-Her-Name, that woman who shot Andy Warhol in 1968. Then they bulldozed the goddamn building in 1971, and sent the not-so-lucky ones to Rikers Island. Those bums, the mayor and his lousy bums, I mean. It was miserable, those days. 'Who could stand looking at an empty lot of junk?' We hollered. We have this garden here finally, after all that hollering."

It was the ghost of the Women's House of Detention — taken down before the garden was built — that seemed the only real thing in this long, drawn-out tribute, against the backdrop of Faith's "followers," the cameras set up to record the day's readings and bits of Faith's poetry shared in solemn tribunals.

I recognized the writer, Amanda Weinstein, holding court by the white magnolias. Her hair clipped perfect as a model, loose-fitting clothes on a lithe body. I watched as Amanda Weinstein — who had been on *The Oprah Winfrey Show* — talked into a microphone about Faith.

I leaned against an oak tree; a magnolia brushed my thigh. Then suddenly, I felt a hand on my arm. "Are you all right?" It was the filmmaker, Esther Kaplan.

"You and I spoke by phone a couple of times; maybe you don't remember with all that's happening," Esther said to me.

She had stopped her camera to acknowledge I was standing in the grass beside her. Taking in my face, she said: "Of course you miss Faith. . ." Despite everything that had passed between us on the phone, Esther Kaplan seemed a warm, earthy woman in sandals, a plain wraparound skirt, and a hippie shirt with threaded patterns.

"There's Don, her husband, I think. Will he be talking soon?"

"I can't say, Esther. I'm sorry," I said, painfully reserved.

"OK, Allegra," Esther placed her hand on my shoulder again. "Are you sure you're all right?" I saw that she was leaning towards me, her mannish face twisted with concern, and quickly I was ashamed for thinking Esther was like all the rest here. It was a kind face, generous. "Of course, this is hell for you, I can see that," Esther said.

"You must be Allegra," a strange woman, running her fingers through her home-cut hair suddenly said. "You knew our Faithie? Well, we're holding vigils, you know. Vigils for Faith."

Esther was pulling up the rest of her camera equipment to protect it against the drizzling rain. She cast a glance at me, and that warmth came back to her face, despite her scramble to pack up her camera equipment.

"I want you to be in my film," Esther said, appearing before me against the declining sun.

"What?" I responded awkwardly.

"The film is all about Faith," Esther said. "Do you have any material? I mean, letters you shared, photos of places you went with her, did you ever witness some of the meetings she had with famous others?"

"Well, yes, sure I do." Now I wished I hadn't stuffed the vitamin bottle full of scotch away. I wanted a sip from it so badly my lips ached.

"Would you be willing to be interviewed?" Esther asked.

"Who is this movie for?" I asked.

"It's for us and posterity," Esther said, "For us who feel a real tribute is needed, a real legacy."

"I'm sorry, I'm not sure. . ."

"Would you come to my apartment this Thursday, and we could talk about it?"

"About what, though?"

"I was calling you. Do you remember — about the film, before?"

"I do," I said. "Yes, I remember."

"I would love it if a student of hers said something; I mean, you were very close to her, I know that. Look, here's my card." Esther whisked out a white card which was slightly soiled. Esther wiped it with her hand, as if embarrassed, but the gesture moved me, moved me to the image of sitting in someone's warm apartment, and talking about Faith. I put my hand in my bag, with the clenched card, my fingers feeling the vitamin bottle of scotch, and I nodded. "I would love that," I said.

"Oh good, oh I'm so glad. I've asked some others. I also asked Faith's best friends, Helen and Jane. I would have loved to ask Susan Sontag. I just would love to hear what Sontag might have said." She moved a distance from me now, as if she had forgotten her camera gear was there on the lawn in the light rain and had to remember to finish packing it. "Look, can you give me your number? I would like to call you, Allegra," she said.

I reached into my bag, and I took out the scotch, reserving it as a secret, thinking of all the secrets I would have to reserve remembering Faith out loud to a stranger. Then, with the vitamin bottle in my left hand and a pen in my right, I wrote my number and name on the slip of newspaper which had the date and time of this tribute on it. It was a page of *The New York Times,* and it had a picture of Faith above the announcement of today's event. I wrote over it, over Faith's face. I wrote my own name and telephone number there and gave it over to the filmmaker. I watched as Amanda Weinstein was walking toward me, her posturing face smiling.

"Thank you," I said to Esther. And then, as Amanda strutted closer to me, I walked very fast to the iron gates, back onto the streets. I did not look back again to see if Amanda had responded to me stealing out or if anybody else had noticed my escape.

By the East River half an hour later, I put my arms over the railing and stared into the muck-brown water. A police tugboat was passing by two ducks — one a dusky female and the other a brightly colored male with blue and green plumage. Both were repeatedly diving down beneath the surface of the river, their heads first, webbed feet up in the swarmy air. I wished I could join them.

I walked back toward a splintered wood bench. I still had a view of the river, but I wasn't able to see the ducks. I fell into an overwhelming sadness and I struggled to pull out of it, to rise to the surface like the ducks. Again, I thought, what if the imprint dissolved?

Now that Faith was no longer there, would it vanish and return me to the hospitals? Who could I tell about this imprint? How could I tell anyone about Faith coming to the hospital that winter in 1973, and testifying to my life, which began my life?

It was here, my brother Julian had agreed to meet with me, to discuss what to do for Sophia, who was losing her dancer's elasticity, and depressed.

I always met Julian wanting to appear happier than I was, and fulfilled, and appreciative of every beat of life. I never wanted to disappoint him as much as I had when he saw me back at Hall Eight after a short visit, his face sinking like an abandoned boy's.

I was careful never to say much about the long-term hospital. I felt his body tense whenever he visited me. Julian had turned into a soft man, usually not accusatory or hostile, much more weight gathered on his six-foot frame, but because he was tall, he wore the weight well. His biggest complaint against me was that, unlike him, I couldn't escape the dark states even now sometimes. It wasn't because it upset him to have a sister who had been in a mental hospital, but because I couldn't see the good in life, he said, the luck we had as wealthy children, and the vast playgrounds in life where the pursuit of human pleasure could have no threshold or limit.

There was Julian nearing the docks from Thirty-Fourth Street; I saw him standing and waiting to cross into the path that would lead him to me. Julian, who did not stay with any lover longer than a year. His wounds were so apparent to me. But he was "happy," he said, and

I believed he had a certain joy and satisfaction with his life, whereby commitment to another was replaced by the pleasures of having many lovers.

I saw him walking through the thick summer air now, his belly not contained by the loose belt around his blue jeans.

"Ha-low!" He said teasingly. "What's happening?"

"Julian. . ." I let him pull me towards his big chest, and I saw the familiar alligator insignia on his shirt; he always wore shirts with alligator insignias, I remembered now, from Bloomingdale's or Brooks Brothers. What I liked about him was how he tried so hard to be "normal," but in conversation was so playful and silly, as if he himself didn't trust his own show. He was going out with a woman with two kids now; he had made love to a man recently who was a middle-aged, spiritual healer whose rap he believed — there was nothing at all about his colorful life that was normal. He lived in Santa Fe, amidst artists and other book designers, and dropouts from Los Angeles or New York.

"So how the hell are you? Let's sit. I need to sit now, puh-lease."

I laughed. "Julian, I'm really fine," I said. Thinking to myself, I haven't seen the inside of a hospital for years, Julian. Please acknowledge this — and if the imprint didn't dissolve. . .

"I wasn't worried." For a few moments, I was silent and studied him. There was a paradox in him; he was a teasing, playful man with charming and sweet ways, but then he would suddenly become afraid of being brought into dark places by me and desperate to get away from me. He could suddenly become aloof and distant.

"Did you come to New York for the book fair?" I asked him now.

"Partly, just partly."

"Did you see Mom?"

"In fact I did, Allegra."

"So we should talk about Mami, the problems that you mentioned on the phone I mean."

"But first, are you writing? Your book did so well. I'm so happy for you and proud of you."

"Yes, a new book."

"Terrific," he said. "That is just so great, I think Mami's doing fine. She's buzzing along and goes out a lot. She has a chauffeur now to take her around to things in Pound Ridge." He stopped. "But, oh no," he said. "Don't put me in the middle between Mom and you. With a sister and mother like that, it's a wonder I like women."

"What a nice thing to say!" I said.

"You know I'm just kidding, sweetie."

"I call Mami once a week, religiously."

"Oh my! Religiously. Me, too. Every Monday night."

"Faith Hale died, you know," I said all of a sudden, shocking myself as much I shocked Julian hearing me speak those words. I wondered if Julian would ever understand my need for Faith. Or what happened, how the imprint had saved my life and I wasn't certified as mentally ill.

Julian bowed his head and drew in a breath. Then: "Oh God, Allegra. I know you were so close to her." He put his arm around my shoulders and squeezed me against him. "Oh, I'm sorry." He said. "Was there a funeral?"

"Not one I was invited to."

"Oh," he said. Then quickly went on. "Mom's okay; I mean, if you're scared for Mom, don't be. Her dancing really kept her body strong. It's just the loss of agility with age. She can't dance like she used to."

I knew I couldn't speak about Faith Hale too much or about the imprint — not to Julian, not to Mami.

"It wasn't the same with Mami after my time in the hospital and those phone calls from the hospital floor," I said.

"Oh, we all forgot already!" Julian said. "How many years ago was that? You couldn't help it. She knows now you couldn't help it, Allegra. You have to understand Mami is very fragile. You called her from a mental hospital, for heaven's sake. Allegra, I told you a thousand times."

"She emotionally disinherited me." I said.

"In a way, maybe, but you were pretty scary those years. It's a long time ago. Can you just move forward for once and not dwell on things?"

This was where I usually stopped liking him, when he said things like that. Sometimes when I tried to talk to him about the hospital, he started teasing me. "It's so deep I cannot reach. . .I can't go there." He would say.

"Sweetie, Mami's has to retire from her dancing," Julian said now. "She can't keep up the estate either now and she loves you. I don't care what you believe. She was sort of frightened of people, of imperfection. She loves control; she needs it. Out-of-control is something she can't handle."

"So are you saying I need to come home and take care of her?" I asked Julian.

"I'm saying there is a time for peace, and maybe this is it."

We sat still and silent for a few minutes, and then I said, "You're right, bro. I should take care of her. Sometimes you are right."

"Hey, let's just watch the river and be quiet now. I will have to go back to Santa Fe, and I don't know when I'll see you again."

After he left, I thought about my brother.

Julian told one story about our childhood over and over again. It was about the time we both got lost in thick woods between two main roads.

"I remember us deciding we were going to walk to Scotts Corners, though it was a long way, and I was uncertain we should do it. But you were the older sister and I wanted to trust you. We came to an intersection and had a big fight on which direction to go. We had gotten lost. And after a while, I allowed myself to be pulled along by you to go in the wrong direction, and all that happened was that we got more and more lost. Luckily, that Halle boy found us there and rescued us."

Clearing my mind about Julian now, I headed back to my apartment.

Chapter Thirteen.

In my apartment an hour later, I decided to go through my file boxes and folders to find something I could give to Esther who was doing the documentary about Faith. The notebooks, about sixteen of them, all from stationary stores, some with fabric covers, some with art designs on the covers, the kind of notebooks one buys in high-end stationary stores where, when you find the first page, it has an emblem that says: "This belongs to—" and you write in your name. There were also so many pens with my notebooks: Montblanc, Waterman, expensive Sheaffers, and vintage Cross pens too.

Everything over the years was good, since Faith took me in and I had showed Faith the notebooks from the streets, and the Prozac my new psychiatrist gave me drew me more and more out of the chaos so that the imprint of Faith could work. It was impossible to know which one played the greater part, the medicine, the notebooks, or Faith's imprint left inside me. Or if it was all because the imprint worked.

I tried to clear my thoughts. I would make Michael's dinner as soon as my head stopped spinning with these thoughts, I thought.

I lay down on the floor. And then I decided to wait for Michael. It would sort out, I thought. Our relationship was so good. Tomorrow was Saturday, dancing at the Copa Cabana tonight with Michael, brunch on Sunday, and lovemaking early Sunday morning. This was because I was well, our "routine." This sweetness was my life in 1988.

I made myself get up now. Diligently, I dressed in my old school jeans and sweaters. I had to force myself; I couldn't stay in this room. Off of the floor I had gathered up some paraphernalia — a letter in Faith's writing on my behalf to the United Nations for research on a book.

Now I went to the closet where I had put a new novel, pages I was drawing out of me about Faith and me, of pulling our story from the depths of memory and debris.

I had stashed a story from *New York* magazine with her other papers. It was a story about a diver who found treasures buried in the East River.

The magazine article said:

> In his day, a man named Barney Swee-ney made newspaper headlines with some of his finds, which included cars, washing machines, and a murder weap-on he found stuck in the branches of a submerged Christmas tree — a pistol that shone there "like an ornament." (*New York* magazine did an article more recently about strange things found in the river.) Submerged in the waters of the river, visibility is low, as sediment clouds the water, and divers would have to go very much by feel. Barney Sweeney would float above the riverbed and probe the mud with a long pole to avoid raising clouds of unsettled muck around him.

Somewhere I read about Barney Sweeney recovering a diamond worth $25,000.

I had been buried once, too. Down below where others hadn't and did not want to know you.

～♀～

Folded into the afternoons in November 2007 was filming at Esther Kaplan's apartment, doing the documentary about Faith Hale. I could not mention the psychiatric hospitalization, the real reason for Faith's presence in my life. When I started to, the word "breakdown" and "hospital" slipping from my lips, Esther had abruptly and quickly cut me off, saying, "I don't have to hear about that."

"You sit here," Esther said the first time I went to her apartment. "Did you think about the notes I gave you?" I went behind the camera, pulling a chair to situate myself.

Eventually I did sit in front of the sixteen-millimeter camera and crossed my legs and felt the hot lights of Esther's studio on my face. Esther Kaplan, equipped with correspondences and stories between her and Faith through the long years after the long-term hospitalization. Esther Kaplan — I went every day to bring sundry paper trails about Faith from my own pile of notebooks. Esther's apartment was a small, crowded place with watercolor paintings on the walls, that looked like the artist had granted them to her as an old lover, abandoning her to this cluttered, manless apartment. Something solitary and sad was reflected in the warm, thick strokes of blue and red paint, as if he had anticipated his departure.

In one of the photos Esther had collected of Faith, Faith was wearing a poncho. It was at Seneca Falls army base: plain pants, and a collared sweater, and as always a pendant dangling from a silver chain onto her breasts over that lovely lavender scarf. Another photo someone had taken of Faith waving from a paddy wagon after she was arrested for climbing over a fence. It was next to a photocopied F.B.I. file started and kept on Faith's doings. Then, left on Esther's couch as if she had needed to study it more closely, was another photo of Faith at an army base in Seneca Falls, holding a poster which read: "We resist the rape of women!"

Most often, though, Esther gave me the feeling that she didn't like me, as if she recognized in me something of herself that she hated, a secret. On those occasions, I let myself fade away.

When called by Esther to a taping, I only sat silently at the table near the kitchen in Esther's apartment in the midst of the documents and photos of Faith, waiting for my turn in front of the camera. I would often feel like one of the objects on the table. Sometimes, I exchanged a few words with the strangers in Esther's apartment, friends of Faith or other interviewees also waiting in Esther's living room for their takes. I liked to appear calmly curious about their lives. My attitude and behavior must have been so courteous and yet so aloof that it would not occur to any of them I had ever been in a mental hospital.

Soon, I stopped going to Esther's at all, telling her I had nothing much else to say.

In my apartment, I walked through the bedroom where I had put my writing before I went to Esther's. This near-desperate feeling of wanting to hold the pages led quickly to me moving into the living room, putting down my yet-indecipherable pages that had already begun a story about Faith. There was the feeling of summer in the apartment, a feeling of warmth and protection and aloneness which I soon realized wasn't because the window was left open, but because Faith was in the room with me. I felt her, as I would, I thought, through the many years to come. I had learned with my father, that death was only a physical loss of voice and body in real time. A few pages describing Faith was on the pages I scribbled in my bedroom after leaving Esther's a few days before: Faith's unruly gray hair, the stocky, loving body that had always moved shoulders first, as if in a march to repair, to rectify something of this world.

I would write Esther a quick note and tell her I would be available for any questions by phone, but I wasn't coming back to the meetings at her house. I couldn't anymore. It was that simple. I wasn't going back to the notion that death was final, either, as I picked up the cheap pen I bought at Walgreen's the day before (after I couldn't find my old one in the mess that had become the living room while Michael was away). The first words on paper felt like a kind of wind that would lead me to an ending of one part of my life. But sure, as a description of her rough but soft body, I had already written: "When I first met Faith Hale, I was nineteen years old and I wanted to be saved. . . ."

Micheal would be home again in two days, and I would tell him. I was writing again. I felt an excitement and a release. Yes, there was proof that the imprint hadn't dissolved. Didn't I see that, feel that? As subtle and quiet as the ending of a long winter season. But it was there. I had Faith.

Acknowledgments

The author would to thank friends and colleagues who stood by her and the book through some difficult times: Caroline Leavitt, Mary Marcus, Lou Aronica, Iris Salomon, and David Skolkin. Huge gratitude to Dr.Mervyn Peskin for help with the often difficult psychological issues in the book, and always to my husband, Matthew Smith for being there, always.

About the Author

Leora Skolkin-Smith was born in Manhattan in 1952, and spent her childhood between Pound Ridge, New York, and Israel, traveling with her family to her mother's birthplace in Jerusalem every three years. She earned her BA and MFA, and was awarded a teaching fellowship for graduate work, all at Sarah Lawrence.

Leora's first published novel, *Edges* (2005), was edited and published by the late Grace Paley for Glad Day Books.

Edges was nominated for the 2006 PEN/ Faulkner Award by Grace Paley; a National Women Studies Association Conference Selection; a Bloomsbury Review Pick, 2006: "Favorite Books of the Last 25 Years"; a Jewish Book Council Selection, 2005; and won the 2008 Earphones Award for an original audio production narrated by Tovah Feldshuh. In addition, it is currently in development as a feature film, produced by Triboro Pictures.

Her novels *The Fragile Mistress* (2008) and *Hystera* (2011) were selected by Princeton University for their series "The Fertile Crescent Moon: Women Writers Writing About Their Past in The Middle East."

Hystera was the winner of the 2012 USA Book Award and the 2012 Global E-books Award. *Hystera* was also a finalist in The International Book Awards, and a finalist in the National Indie Excellence Awards.

Leora was the Director and a teacher for the non-profit organization The Fiction Project for Hospitals, conducting prose workshops for in-patient psychiatric patients. The organization was funded by The New York State Council for the Arts, The Department of Cultural Affairs, Con Edison, and the Patricia Kind Foundation

Leora is a contributing editor to readysteadybook.com, and her critical essays have been published in *The Washington Post*, *The Quarterly Conversation*, The National Book Critic's Circle's *Critical Mass*, and other places.

Leora's fiction has been published in *Guernica, Persea: An International Review, Jewish Fiction,* and other journals.